Dearest Gloria, my best
friend in the whole world.

You were always there for me.
I hope you know how much
your presence meant to me.
I could not have survived
all these years without
your support.

God always brings a light
and you were my light in so
many days of darkness.
moreover you were beside me
doing God's work.
I love you and always will
my dearest and bestest
friend in the whole world.
Nirmala.

Do Not
Look Back to When
You Held On—
and Let Go

Eileen Ponammah

authorHOUSE®

AuthorHouse™
1663 Liberty Drive
Bloomington, IN 47403
www.authorhouse.com
Phone: 1-800-839-8640

Published by AuthorHouse 05/22/2014

ISBN: 978-1-4969-0950-3 (sc)
ISBN: 978-1-4969-0951-0 (hc)
ISBN: 978-1-4969-0952-7 (e)

Library of Congress Control Number: 2014907987

Any people depicted in stock imagery provided by Thinkstock are models,
and such images are being used for illustrative purposes only.
Certain stock imagery © Thinkstock.

This book is printed on acid-free paper.

Because of the dynamic nature of the Internet, any web addresses or links contained in
this book may have changed since publication and may no longer be valid. The views
expressed in this work are solely those of the author and do not necessarily reflect the
views of the publisher, and the publisher hereby disclaims any responsibility for them.

For those who are suffering or have suffered abuses of any type, as a child or an adult. You are not alone; others go before you and more will come after you. This book is dedicated to you so that your pain and suffering is acknowledged and validated. It is hoped that you make the step-by-step process of healing, a journey from victim to survivor to enjoy living a life of your own.

For my father and my mother, rest in peace.

Contents

Acknowledgements

I smile with pride when I think of the people who have come into my life for an awakening, to give me the truth, to guide me, to listen from a distance as a voice at the end of the phone, to share a meal when I was lonely, and to offer a helping hand and half a laborious task. Others have come on the journey as companions for the road, and their presence is ever felt. But only a few, despite their heavy crosses, have the generosity of spirit to help the other.

It is in the utmost respect and gratitude that I hold these "helpers," who shall remain anonymous but not faceless. At times, people have helped me when I was not aware I was even being helped. My helping angels have never faltered and, though weathered and beaten by life, stand tall as helpers throughout eternity – lifelong givers. These helpers shared moments of strife and moments of joy. If a round of gunfire in salute to your souls and energy were possible, you would all have it and more.

Preface

This book is written with the intention of helping people who are suffering from mental, emotional, physical, and sexual abuse. It is inspirational, in that it shows a woman's struggle to rise above toxic relationships and defend her mental health. It is hoped that psychiatrists, lawyers, and counsellors come together to understand the complex dynamics of "sinister secrets", "lies", "blaming", and "shame". The author will turn to art to express and capture feelings that she cannot fully do justice; you will find references borrowed from art to illustrate the depth and gravity of her suffering.

The author turns to masterpieces like Patrick Hamilton's play *Gaslight*; *Cruel Intentions*, directed by Roger Kumble; *Secrets and Lies*, a 1996 British film directed by Mike Leigh; Harper Lee's novel, *To Kill a Mocking Bird*; and a play by J. B. Priestley called *An Inspector Calls*. She also references songs such as Michael Bublé's "I Wanna Go Home" and "Wide Awake" by Katy Perry. Great works of art can freeze a moment, capturing and truthfully communicating the intensity of an emotion or the banality of ordinariness. It is hoped that this book will help families who have to deal with sexual, emotional, mental, and physical abuses. The reader will obviously see the damage done to individuals when family and community bury their heads, cruelly neglecting the emotional and mental pain of the victim. It is not just the victims themselves who suffer, others involved suffer too.

The games people play in the name of family honour are questionable when weighed against human pain and suffering. Children who are victims of sexual abuse, physical abuse, and emotional/mental abuses have deep mental scars. Mental cruelty, like physical abuse, is prevalent and real. Victims of hidden sexual abuse create a tsunami, pulling casualties along with them when the dark and light sides of human nature are caught in a system that does not allow victims to seek help, especially when the perpetrators are family members. Abuse can scar you permanently and, left untreated, can wreck lives. The damage is real and lasting. This book is a call for all professionals, psychiatrists, counsellors, chiropractors, naturopathic doctors, and lawyers to help break the system of unitary work and replace it with something more collaborative. Everyone or anyone interested can unite, as stakeholders in "the business of saving" the abused, whether they are sexually, mentally, emotionally, or physically abused.

The abused is damaged and will unconsciously become the destroyer. Soon, the victim will be the one holding the gun under orders of his or her family. When the abuser has long gone, victims are still struggling against a family system that does nothing to help.

Idhaya Tagore, the principal character in this story, lived with a victim of sexual, mental, and physical abuse. Idhaya was not sexually abused, yet she wanted to stand and shout, "I was mentally and emotionally abused, a fallout of the act against a child."

Idhaya came into her new family as a naive angel; her path was not an easy road, and she transformed into a devil. She walked two sides, the good and the bad. As self-defence, she retaliated with a higher level of cruelty than that which was done unto her. She didn't start out as vindictive and cruel, but when her family was trying to destroy her mentally in order to keep their dark sinister secrets, she retaliated and became just as cruel. Whether her reaction was self-defence, retaliation, revenge, or vindictiveness, she did not really know; all she knew was that her reaction was instinctual. She did not like what she was becoming, but the change in her was a survival instinct; a trapped animal fighting against a pack will always bring out the animal in the human being.

Idhaya fought to defend herself against lies and to prove that she was sane when family honour was at stake. The family opened a can of worms that they would live to regret. Suddenly she found herself facing a family secret that brought into question what she thought she knew to be true. Who was her son, Kumar's, real grandmother? Idhaya doubted what she heard, and her family attempted to convince her that her experiences were hallucinatory. Idhaya's eldest sister had taken her own life, and her younger brother had been diagnosed with schizophrenia.

Idhaya's fears were real. She feared a repeat of a family illness in herself. Her husband's web of deceit shook the very foundation of her marriage and all her understanding of family, religion, race, and culture. The in-laws perfect alibi was her sensitivity to human suffering and pain. She would replay the mantras of "sticks and stones will break my bones, but names will never hurt me" and "walk through life and not against it", almost as if these mantras would make it easy for her to live her life. She repeated these mantras when her husband not only colluded with the family but also was the instigator in maintaining the secrets at the expense of his and her own mental health.

Family honour was at stake – an honour built on lies and hypocrisy. In actuality, the conspiracy theory her husband attempted to sell her was an attempt to convince Idhaya that she was as crazy as her brother; it was an excuse to cover up the reasons for the cruelty in the family – why they were so bitter and judgmental. Their dark and sinister secrets only meant that the family stayed close and no one was allowed in the inner sanctum; there were always a "them" and an "us" – the outlaws versus the in-laws or rather those who were privy to the information.

She wanted to leave her marriage but not without her child. She knew the clan would only let her leave if she did so alone. A Pandora's box opened and allowed her to walk with her child. The family she left behind was damaged goods, outwardly respectable but damaged, and they, like the tsunami, left Idhaya emotionally battered, bitter, and weather-worn from the knocks she'd received.

Art so often imitates life. Idhaya, who was "falling from cloud nine", realised that her life was a psychological horror movie. Her in-laws were trying to destroy her mentally and emotionally and have her sectioned in a loony bin. She knew that the family cared more for keeping their dark secrets than they did for her health. And if she stayed long enough, they would have her believe that she needed a straitjacket, and she would march herself into the mental hospital.

She was mentally free to raise her child and not believe the press by the in-laws – that she was a bad or unfit mother. Whoa!

Her initial choice for freedom from her own dysfunctional family opened when her father died. Yet she ignored the signs that there was nothing real between her future husband and herself. She accepted an arranged marriage. Her single choice for a shot at life became a consequence – an entrapment – and she was stuck in a nightmarish life. How this choice would finally play out was ultimately uncanny and reminiscent of a Hitchcock ending. Life's slapstick comedy and irony can be shocking. Comedy and tragedy are juxtaposed, so that the reader can find solace in suffering.

The gradient grey of mental illness and Idhaya's diagnosis of schizo-affective disorder gave her new family a perfect alibi to hide their shame and their dark sinister secrets. She would question her diagnosis when she attended marriage counselling. The continual lies and creeping self-doubt destabilised her mental state and threatened to propel her further into her named psychosis. Her fight for freedom will leave the reader believing there is hope in darkness. In the end, two choices availed themselves to her – (1) to stay depressed and live in fear or (2) to leave her marriage and toxic relationships for a shot at mental freedom and happiness.

All that awaited her was the unknown. Idhaya only knew that what she was leaving was far more destructive than facing the unknown. It was the second time in her life that she made a decision to face unfamiliar territory.

This time, the choice (to stay ill or leave a failed marriage) opened when her mother passed away. Idhaya did not know what awaited her, only that, to be healthy enough for herself and to raise her child, she must face society with a new tag – "the divorcee". This would now be her new reality.

Living in all these chronic conditions, Idhaya was also physically affected by stress hormones. This was the result of years of living in a psychologically abusive relationship where her husband would fly into rages that appeared to be getting worse with age. The initial shock of having to live with this rage did not wane. The years were a sentence – shackled to a marriage of mental abuse, shackled by culture and by religion – and not just for Idhaya but Andrew, her husband. He was wound so tightly. Idhaya suspected that her husband probably had attention deficit disorder like her son. Everything was delayed until it was a fire. He was a compulsive liar and frustrated at having to live a lie.

When Idhaya left her marriage, her physical ailments lessened. Her irritable bowel syndrome, endometriosis, and arthritis all decreased; she was no longer experiencing stress at a high level of eight and was now at a level three. Whoa!

Andrew suffered from diabetes, and the stress of maintaining secrets and lies had taken its toll. It was visibly written on his face. He was given his freedom by her decision to leave, and thus, his suffering was alleviated too.

There is a happy ending, but it is outside of conformity and repressions that constrain behaviour and dictate moral codes. Do not be fooled by stereotypes – the great illusion. We lose so much of the richness of a human being if we base our understanding of a person on stereotypes, which is a false consciousness. Go beyond stereotypes to find universal shared truths. We can, in the end, live fully in the essence of "self" beyond family, race, religion, and culture. Our unique self does not need to please or appease society, family, or community. We have strength within, but they face the paradox of looking externally for strength, which in the end is in us all, an internal journey of self-discovery. Our duty is to our essence of self. A self, unlike the "holy grail" in *The Fisher King*, starring Robin William, is a search for truth, peace, love, and acceptance as part of human need. The movie is not just about a destitute wounded homeless man who believes himself to be on a quest for the holy grail but a powerful story of one person with a purpose greater than himself.

Our parents, our caregivers become controllers who, in the end, incarnate a system of brainwashing that overlooks the essence of self, and what we are left with is an internal conflict of an adult who begs to be a human trophy for his or her parent. Idhaya's husband was a tortured soul, frustrated and angry at the burden of becoming a human trophy for his family, for his parents. The lesson that we must carpe diem (seize the day) in the film *Dead Poets Society* should not be overlooked.

The Five Coins in the Water

This is my story. I am Idhaya Tagore, a free-spirited, South Indian Tamil woman with brownish hair. My grandfather, a Hindu astrologer with a King George dignified beard, neatly combed, chose my name. It is a name derived from the Sanskrit language and he chose it by checking the stars. I am nothing like my name spontaneous and happy-go-lucky. I have been told that a person's name is one of the most beautiful sounds to their ear. Over the years, the Chinese, the English, the French and others have tried to pronounce my name with fluidity. I rather prefer the way the French say my name, placing the correct emphasis – they make my name sound pleasing and beautiful. I have often wondered if I am like my mother or like my father in some shape or form. I am not at all tall in stature, only five feet tall. And, as a teenager, I wore the Nana Mouskouri magnifying eyeglasses; thankfully, my two other sisters, Fathima and Hamza, had the same. As a child, I was rather ordinary, mousy in comparison to my four other siblings; as a wallflower and an observer, I was deeply analytical. I was not truly a participant in fun or life – just a role player and a pleaser. I was forever and a day bottling things up, all the storms and the rainy days, and weathering the journey. While my life was calm, I still walked on eggshells in anticipation of the storm.

I was born in Ipoh, Malaysia. I grew up in a terraced house in Ladbroke Grove, London, England, during the late '70s, '80s, and '90s, where the roads were narrow and everyone was forced to park on the streets. Driving in the streets of London was a test of one's ability and agility. The one lane was used as a two-way passing, where cars met bumper-to-bumper, kissing headlights and grazing wing mirrors.

Papa was working at the English military base in Singapore as a civilian when both he and his brother were made redundant. Ammah and the children were living in Malaysia and at that time, the government of Singapore was not allowing Malaysian family citizens to come and live their husbands. Papa also wanted the family to stay together. I suspect, though I am not 100% certain, Papa's redundancy became a catalyst for his decision to immigrate to England. Whether Papa's motivation was singular or a culmination of reasons, Papa decided to try his luck in England – the walk of survival. Papa's unspoken desire was that his children would be professionals among the A-list of accountants and lawyers, possibly even pilots. What he failed to realise was that his decision alone to emigrate was only a seed. The five pebbles thrown into the river were given the strategy that you either learnt to swim or you drowned. I and my siblings grew up with the same Ammah and Papa, but like the five fingers on one hand, we were all so different.

We were the dark mocha, chocolate, and espresso complexion; there were no skinny latte complexions in this household. Ammah and Papa's children were the proverbial five coins in the Trevi Fountain, each on a journey like no other, each with a wish for his or her life that the others could not understand.

In Malaysia at five-year-old I would run to the tall iron gate and wait for the postman to deliver letters from my father in England. Soon I would face him.

❦ ❦ ❦

The plane journey from Malaysia to England was filled with the enthusiasm of small children on an adventure, not perceptive enough to appreciate that this trip was going to change our lives. We ran up and down the gangway, annoying the air hostess, who told us to go back and sit down in our seats. Balram, the eldest son, was given a toy airplane by the relatives, and he bothered Ammah with his fears that the plane was going to crash. Fathima, my eldest sister, and I each had an orange teddy bear to keep us quiet for the long flight. Nevertheless, it was more fun to run up and down the gangway annoying the air hostess, and Ammah's resolve was calm and silent, even though Abijan, the baby was crying.

Papa and his long-standing Singaporean friend came to the airport at London, Heathrow with jackets for us. It was a dark and cold November night, and Papa wanted to put me on his lap; he wanted to be close to his children. But his year alone in England was long. I faced a stranger.

Ammah and we children tried to recover the gap year.

Papa didn't waste any time in registering us for school. We dressed in front of the electric fire and walked twenty minutes to get to get to local primary and middle school. At school, the children thought it was funny that I could not pronounce "film" but would always say "felim" with a singsong accent – "la, la, la", a remnant of my time in Malaysia and Singapore. At school, my new friends and I would play black jacks and marbles in the school playground. I had a collection of cat's eyes marble and kept them in a jar. All the school children had a small bottle of milk, it was the era of the Thatcher years – free milk for us. Tracey, my best friend and I would skip school and go swimming at the local public swimming pool only to be caught by a teacher of another school.

As a child, I wished I could go "back home" to Malaysia. Each time I heard a plane fly overhead, I would run to the window and look at the sky. Papa would quietly and calmly watch on the sidelines. He wrote letters to his father in Singapore saying that the children were homesick and wanted to go back. Ammah never really showed us that she missed Malaysia or her family, the only thing she ever revealed to me much later on in Canada was that "she never gave so much problems to Papa as I did to my husband" but then she was not being mentally abused or living with the flare ups of a repressed rage. Papa was cool-headed, understated in his manner until his patience was worn thin.

It was only when I was twenty-three years old and I could afford my airfare to go to Singapore and Malaysia that I realized that "back home": did not exist anymore; the years spent in England had made England home. Singapore was going through a courtesy kindness campaign with Singa-lion emblem I did not realize that time had passed and I had changed. I visited the parrot lady in Little India Serangoon Road and asked for my future. She was a Tamil lady and a tourist attraction. My cousin told me to be quiet so that she could barter for the cheap fake watches, if I opened my mouth, I would be a dead-giveaway as a tourist. I enjoyed eating at the Hawker stalls, the open-air food court where you can buy and eat under the sun from a choice of Malay, Indian and Chinese cuisine. No one seemed to care if you went out with your sarong or house clothes. At the end of my holiday, I said good-bye to a yearning I had since my childhood of "back-home". The nostalgia and sentimentality of "back home" had been replaced with an awakening and a consciousness of my acceptance of a new home country.

🦋 🦋 🦋

Years living in London in the same red-bricked black mortar house with a small black iron gate an overgrown green privet hedge, meant that I knew the neighbours; the pharmacists; the Muslim corner shopkeeper, Iqbal; and the English local chippy owner who used to serve fish and chips wrapped in newspaper back in the days. Our streets were tree lined and the houses were from the Victorian and Edwardian times. You see, London was not such an unfriendly place, where everyone walked with an umbrella in anticipation of the rain. I would watch the neighbours' children grow up and have their own children; I would witness how one drama after another would unfold in their lives, just like fiction. As if they were living out the London soap *Coronation Street*, someone had cancer and someone was having an affair, and then there was the wayward teenager. I would be unwaveringly protective of England, my adopted country, and would be defensive if anyone tried to denigrate England.

Papa was smart enough to rent the three bedrooms of the house he'd bought during his first year in England. The rent was only a meagre five pounds a week. Each bedroom had a gas meter, and the tenants could slot in their coins for heating. An old Victorian fireplace in the living room and one in the upstairs bedroom gave the house a sense of time and life. All three tenants had to share the pokey upstairs kitchen and bathroom. There was Gopal, who drew naked women; a Japanese student called Sugi who worked in Kentucky Fried Chicken; and a Japanese international student, Yesoko, who worked part-time in Donuts Diner. We were lucky, as children, whenever it was our birthdays; we'd get a bucket filled with fried chicken and a box of donuts, and we felt rich, rich, rich.

It was a free-for-all when I was young. Everyone, including the tenants, could get on the bandwagon and give us a scolding. I would pack my clothes in plastic bags ready to run away from home whenever this happened, but neither Papa nor Ammah took my running away seriously, and there I would sit at the foot of the stairs.

Ammah befriended the tenants and turned the other way when they could not afford to pay the rent. Ammah lacked a worldly savvy for life, believing the religious brainwashing that one was to accept everything without complaining. Her eyes were tilted to the heavens.

As children, the streets were the playgrounds, and my siblings and I dodged the cars, skipped outside the house, and knocked hard on their neighbours' houses and ran away with a mischievous glee. When the neighbours' children returned the favour, Papa would stand behind the front door waiting to catch them in the act. A cricket ball was thrown at one of the neighbour's windows, and Papa made harsh grumbling noises about how he had to pay for the folly of Balram, the eldest son. The alleys at the back of the house, with stray cats and small gardens, were reminiscent of the soap *Coronation Street*. Prince, the family's cat, would always come when the theme song came on, and he too sat watching the soap. We could have fun on the streets. When Princess Diana and Prince Charles got married it was just that, a street camaraderie, where everyone joined in to celebrate the marriage, waving Union Jack flags and eating ham and cheese sandwiches and sausage rolls and drinking canned fizzy drinks.

The walks through Portobello Market and Shepherds Bush Market and the little old lady who read our palm were some of my earliest memories of London. Getting served in the market was not always first come, first served; one had to be pushy to get served. The dealers came to sell their wares and antiques. My friend Bethany's father was the artful dodger. He could never understand how the service repairman could hoodwink his daughter by charging a high price to "fix" a boiler that was beyond repair. Surely, she should have seen it coming. "You ain't no daughter of mine!" he said.

London had a life all of its own, never boring; a bus ride to the West End was filled with a thrill. The street life, with buskers and musicians, comic sketches and dance mimes were all free entertainment for the passers-by. Countless international students, foreign businessmen and women, and travellers from all over the world were lured to London. Some made it their stopgap, made their money and left, and others felt that you could never have enough of London and stayed for the long haul, watching their pennies for day to day living. London was expensive.

In my youth, my siblings and I would go to the Notting Hill Carnival, which was street life at its best, a metropolitan and cosmopolitan city coming alive, with smells of West Indian food, jerk chicken, rice and peas, and fried chicken. Years later, I could still taste the mouth-watering fried chicken, my favourite. As children, we felt the fear and went to see the carnival with the colourful costumes of the performers and followed the sounds of the steel bands echoing down the streets. London was alive, with a vibe all its own. A pulse of energy filled the air.

Piccadilly Circus was an urban secret garden with an entrée of excitement by every corner, an awe of the unexpected, the boldness and roughness of London daring newcomers to go the distance. Walking the streets of London was the march of the ants, as it was swamped with tourists and regular commuters who would take the double-decker buses, the London Underground or British Rail trains. The homeless never slept because London was this den of iniquity, where unwelcome trouble could be found on the streets in bold light of day or in the darkness of the night.

Many years later, I would work either in the West End or the East End of London, and being packed like sardines in a can was part of the norm for the commute to work; commuters tried to read their folded newspaper and avoided eye contact when friend or foe came face-to-face. The daily perfume of body odour in a tightly packed carriage was all part of the service when you paid your fare. Whiffs of strange smells in the air were obligatory. In two or six minutes, the next train would arrive, but no one wanted to wait, and commuters pushed and pushed to get into the carriage for rush, rush, and rush hour. Stepping toes, umbrella and briefcases pokes, and bomb scares were just part of the norm of the commuting experience.

🦋 🦋 🦋

Ammah and Papa were Hindus, and we children were raised under the umbrella, partly as Hindus. Then, when I was nine years old, Ammah decided to convert the family to Catholicism. Ammah was raised in a convent in Malaysia and aspired to be a religious nun, but her father, a staunch Hindu, forbade this with his own motto, "Born a Hindu, die a Hindu". Ammah loved Jesus and vowed that, if her gallstones were healed, she would convert the family. Ammah was healed. She took her time about the conversion, until her sister affirmed that, once you made a vow to God, you must keep it. Ammah, with her oversized bottom, sat on a small wooden chair made for schoolchildren and took her religious instruction. After her baptism, Papa and we children all followed suit, and the whole family converted. For Papa, he went with the flow, attending church masses late and leaving early. He regularly stayed at the back of the church for a quick getaway.

Whenever I accompanied Ammah to church, it was always a long walk. The parishioners of St Joseph's Church would ask Ammah for prayers and tell her their heart-wrenching stories. As the years rolled on, soon these parishioners became the supportive extended family Ammah needed. Ammah would stop and introduce me to everyone she met, and she blessed and thanked them for the smallest of deeds. What some might consider a weakness of character was actually Ammah's strength. Ammah would repeatedly come to the front door as I left for work. At Ammah's funeral, Hamza's eulogy spoke of this characteristic. Ammah not only blessed Hamza but me too. Ammah straightened my collar as if I was nine years old. She never grew bored or tied of this habit, and it continued even as we children matured. She would not take us shopping for clothes or jewellery or cosmetics; it was never within her scope. Ammah was always preoccupied with other things. Ammah focussed not on what was lacking; she only appreciated what was done for her. It was infuriating really! An equally worthless and pointless pursuit was engaging Ammah in gossip, because she could never get the story straight and would mix up the characters, which could be potentially dangerous. She did not want to see the flaws of people and had her own motto: "If you point a finger at another person, three point back at you."

Throughout Ammah's life, she would continue to sprinkle holy water and holy salt around the beds, every morning and night. She went to 9.30 a.m. Mass every day at the local Catholic church, visiting all the saints and burning candles and would stop at St Jude, who was there for the hopeless cases, the last saint at the back of the church, closest to the door. She said, "Whenever you visit a new church, you have to light a candle and make three wishes."

I would sing in the church choir, purposely standing beside a girl called Ginette, who had the most amazing voice. I imitated her and kept up with the high notes. As a soprano, at times, my voice sounded nasal. I loved singing and felt that it kept me close to an essence of spirituality. I never learned to read music, but music was like "being in love" or perhaps it is exactly like the poem *I know why the caged bird sings* by Maya Angelou, a liberating experience. Years later, I would discover that my spirit could align with a Muslim, a Christian, a Hindu, and a Buddhist who were here to help lift any cross one might bear.

Papa worked in Dagenham Ford Factory in the assembly line, and the commute was a tiresome journey from the West End of London to the East End. Papa used to work shifts. He would work through the night and then sleep during the day, and consequently, we rarely interacted with him. We were hushed and instructed to keep the noise level down so he could sleep. Slowly, he became the ghost figure walking through the corridors and into rooms, silently observing his family. Looking back into the past, I would later see this particular moment as if he was never home.

I would cut my father's hair, and the bald eagle would sit silently on the chair, fold his arms, and cross his legs. Chewing my tongue in the corner of my left cheek in deep deliberate concentration, I took less than five minutes to trim the wispy hair that poked out at the back of his neck and the small thinning cowlick.

The '70s saw Ford Motor Company employees strike for better pay, and Papa was also on the picket line. Papa's face was in the newspaper, a smart-looking man with a cigarette in his hand and his 1950's well-worn leather jacket and a heavy cumbersome silver wristwatch. Papa was not a risk-taker and did not challenge himself. He played his cards safe all his life. He joined Ford Factory, and in those days, you stayed as a lifer. To stay for a regular pay cheque in a mundane job – not to be swayed by a dream – had to take some sacrifice. Papa was one of the oldest factory workers, and he earned the nickname "Ghandi" from his young factory co-workers.

He bought us blue Ford anoraks, and as children, we wore them with pride in support of Papa's workplace. Papa told Balram, "Do not aim for the coconut but the stars; don't be a factory worker like me. Do better." This was his advice to his eldest son, who had to confront the fact that, by virtue of being the firstborn, he was trapped and condemned to a fate of servitude. It was a love/hate job being the firstborn, for sure. He had his own desire to leave and abandon the sinking ship, but the tentacles of family kept a tight stranglehold on him.

Papa was a quiet man and a defender of the weak. Or maybe just maybe he believed his own line, "You do not need to play music to a deaf and dumb audience." He was hard to understand, hard to love, and I looked upon my father as the brown Marlboro man, a Marlon Brando mixed with Buddy Holliday. He kept the swastika from the days of the Japanese occupation in Singapore and his leather jacket. These articles were kept mostly out of sentiment of his bygone youthful days. He had albums filled with memories of a past, his ballroom dancing days, his different hairdos, his motorcycle, and his pride and joy – his family. These spanned the years, but he rarely looked at them, to remember that once upon a time, he had been young, good-looking, and a contender for a street fight.

Papa was a gambler with a well-worn "poker face"; whether he had won or lost was never written on his face. He would go to the bookies, Ladbroke Grove, at the top of the road and choose the winning horse. He also played the Vernon football pools and would cut up all the numbers on pieces of paper and put them in a jar. As children, we would take turns shaking the bottle, hoping the winning the numbers would miraculously fall out. Prince, had a go too, walking on the numbers.

Once, he won close to nine hundred pounds, and he bought a long pine dining table, benches, and a matching buffet. Now the family could have dinners together and conversations that kept us all amused. Ammah had an open-house policy, and friends of the family came unannounced and uninvited but were fed. Those who gathered at the house were a mixed bag of people; men and women were never divided, and a mishmash of all races and ages were present.

Balram's friends became Fathima's friends; Fathima's friends became my friends, and my friends became Hamza's friends. There were no tea parties or bridge or card games with the people who came to our house. We talked about everything and had a light-hearted sense of humour of the silly type, the clowning of Charlie Chaplin's slapstick comedy rather than the smart wit. As teenagers, Gillian and I would drink and bellow at passers-by, taking turns pushing each other in a shopping trolley. Gillian was my longstanding friend from when I was fifteen years old with a vivacious love of life. We grew up together. We played rounder on the estates using my toddler cousins as posts. They were moving targets still in nappies at that time, hardly solid posts.

When Papa bought the first black-and-white television without a remote control, I thought I was the only one to own a television. I went to school to tell my friends and was shocked to learn that televisions were in most homes. There were BBC 1, BB2, and ITV, and then came along Channel 4; these were the family's only medley of channels. After the 9.00 p.m. BBC news, it was bedtime for the children, though once or twice, we snuck downstairs.

Luckily, Papa's Indian friend Raju was a repairman and he would come regularly with his Irish wife to repair the blinking television when slapping it did not work. In those days, no one ever threw anything out. Things around the house were just repaired and never replaced, and it was not the era for the upgrade. In those days, progress was not really trying to be ahead of time.

In the early days, Ammah would wash everyone's clothes by hand with a cake of soap in the bathtub and hang them to dry on the clothesline in the backyard. The shirt collars never seemed whiter. Once she had the washing machine, she would make the trip to the local laundrette with a black bag of wet clothes to dry them in the enormous industrial dryer or use the clothesline at the back of the house, depending upon the weather.

As a child, I remembered Papa eating ice cream – real ice cream – while my siblings and I had ice pops. I resented that, felt it was selfish on his part. But honestly, that was the only thing I can remember Papa buying for himself. The memory impacted me so. Through the eyes of a child, Papa enjoying his special treat seemed a huge crime. How dare Papa have an ice cream when we were eating ice pops? It was an odd impression of a moment that stuck in my mind even after his death.

Another childhood memory lodged in the past was when I stepped on an ant deliberately and stubbornly. I could have avoided this. The desire was not necessarily to hurt or kill the helpless ant but a nonchalant attitude, a *so what if I do.* I regretted and felt guilty for this. As I grew, I would swat the bothersome blue arse flies and keep a jar of sweetened water – a mix of oil, sugar, and lemon – to catch the annoying fruit flies. I became hardened to the road, a far cry from the child who lamented over harming that which was already weak, dying or smaller than me. I would have similar conversations with my own son about being cruel and making the choice to enhance life rather than destroying it. It fell on deaf ears too. I knew he was too young to comprehend, but over time, I hoped he would.

Years later, my mother-in-law in Sri Lanka would show me the ruins of her father's house, as if it was still a vibrant palace. As she turned to me and banged on her chest for emphasis, she said, "You see, I was somebody." We are all somebody, something of value, no matter how small. It was not a testimony of one's strength but of one's weakness to hurt or harm that which is weak and dying.

It was Christmas all over again. This year, Papa had placed a larger present than ever under the tree, and we children all eyeballed the single present for days. None of us were allowed to touch or open it. I thought about how nice it would be if I could be the one to get that present or could at least know what was inside. We were all curious kittens.

Papa gave the gift wrapped box to his friend's son, who was recovering in hospital after a car accident. My Christmas present was a bottle of bubble bath and a pair of tights. Fathima and Hamza got the same, just possibly a different scent. I surely remembered Papa smirking. Trick or treat. More like trick.

On another day, after a childish episode, the details of which escape me, Papa slapped me. Later, Papa wanted to be forgiven, and out came the Freeman's catalogue and he asked me what I wanted to buy. I wanted the famous cat suit with the Charlie's Angels badge, the famous crime drama where women were the epitome of strength. I stubbornly refused his peace offering. Forgiveness was not my strong point. I looked at the cat suit, and though I liked it, not forgiving my father and making him feel the sting of my anger was more important. I never really said sorry for this deliberate "slap in the face". The childish ordinary rebuke that meant nothing at the time would later seem significant, though Papa would have forgotten my anger.

Things went weirdly wrong in the household when Abijan, the fourth child, the thorny troublesome son, had his breakdown at eighteen and was sectioned in St Bernard's Hospital in Ealing. I was on holiday in Malaysia, and my friend met me at the airport in Heathrow, London: "Sad what happened to Abijan. Not nice news to come home to."

I visited my younger brother. I had to go through two doors, and Abijan's new temporary home seemed like a maximum security at a prison and not a hospital. Abijan was playing table tennis with another patient, and as he hit the ball, he would say, "I cannot see the ball."

I sat opposite him. His beard was overgrown, and his hair long and unkempt. He said in a daze, "You are my sister. I thought you died."

Everything was taken out of his room, even the mirror; only a bed remained in his bare room. In his drawer, I found torn bits of paper and thought, *Why on earth would he do this and keep it there?*

A few days later, he tried to escape with just his pyjamas and headed for the bus stop, hoping to catch, no doubt, the 83 bus home. Abijan was being drugged; he had a comatose look.

Introspectively, looking back, it was hard to explain or come to terms with why Abijan had a breakdown and why he was diagnosed with schizophrenia. I recollected his childhood, recalled Abijan, a snotty-nosed child, wearing three-quarter pants even though it was not fashionable. He would use the wooden Popsicle sticks as a pretend gun. He needed help adjusting to school. Abijan definitely had a knack for attracting trouble, being misunderstood by his peers and teachers alike. He lagged behind in his schoolwork, as he was having difficulty listening to instructions and I have often wondered whether he had a learning difficulty. He could not hear as a child and had had to undergo surgery to rectify the problem. As a teenager, he would break dance with his friends on the streets and would walk around with his ghetto blaster. Abijan's world and mine were poles apart. He was focused and trying every day. Overlooked and ignored by the system, he struggled to bridge the gap of what he knew and did not know. He could not spell "extinguisher" as an adult but he could string a wonderful metaphor when he wrote, "I have a scratch of a tiger, and I can't go back to the land of my forefathers." In reality, Abijan had a tattoo on his left shoulder of a tiger.

Ammah wanted the family together for Christmas and to have her son there. Gillian, my friend for my journey in life, was the voice at the hospital that begged for his temporary release. Gillian had lustre for life but more importantly, she had a knack to befriending the mentally ill and kept her phone lines free. She had a broad shoulder for everyone. That year, it was a Christmas story of a different kind, tinged with sadness, celebrating the temporary release of my brother, who did not know who he was, let alone who his family members were. Our interactions were never the same again.

Finally, Abijan returned home from hospital permanently; there were many fights and loud music well into the early morning. I wondered how the neighbours ever slept and why they never complained. During one fight, Fathima broke her finger, and during another, Abijan tried to throw me over the banisters. Ammah, Fathima, Hamza, and I ran to Hamza's bedroom and locked the door. I called from the window of Hamza's bedroom to a passing neighbour, who promptly called the police. The policeman came and told Abijan to calm down. In the kitchen, we found he had pulled the cutlery drawer out and had taken a knife. He did not intend it. It was just outside of his mind's control.

The stress was constant, and the family all worried for Ammah. Abijan learnt to live and cope with his illness by going to the gym and following his own path as a gifted rapper. I saw my brother piece together a broken mind, and he learnt to walk independently outside the confines of society. I witnessed him hearing voices telling him to do certain things. "I am possessed by the devil," he would say. These statements exasperated Ammah, who would get the holy water and then call Father Stephen Leonard, a call for help and for prayers. I felt that these displays were merely an attempt to provoke a reaction from Ammah. *Did he not know Ammah loved Jesus?* It was difficult for any of us to sleep a restful sleep. The aggravating loud music would have Ammah go upstairs to his bedroom and knock hard on the door, saying: "Abi darling, turn the music down."

🦋 🦋 🦋

Hamza, the youngest, was crying out for love, Ammah used to say. Hamza was the London baby conceived in England; she knew no other country. When Abijan became ill and so far removed from us all, Hamza felt the attention go away from her. To be fair, an elder sick brother overshadowed her all her life, and it became understandable why Hamza, the baby, craved and carved a life for herself, developing her own motto, which was "me, me, and me". She was a survivor and grew up on her own. She was the youngest and a prima donna – tall, slim, confident, and attractive. Being five foot six was an admirable quality in the looks department, more in tune to the world's image of beauty than the shorter stature of Ammah, Fathima, and me.

In later life, Hamza would marry and have her own children. She loved her children and was fortunate enough to have Ammah there as a pulse in the house to make sure that everything went smoothly. Hamza was not really a stay-tied-behind-the-kitchen-sink mother, and to be fair, neither was I. To the outside world, Hamza was single-handedly running her family home. She had an entourage of helpers, picking up her dirty clothes, ironing, cleaning her house, doing the shopping, gardening, and babysitting. I felt a certain type of resentment because Hamza never shared Ammah. Hamza was free to have a life. In the end, I had to accept that my path was that of the lone champion, and maybe God knew I was stronger than I thought, though many times I felt I could not fight alone. Abijan would remind me that I'd always fought for him at school when there were bullies. I drew strength from this.

Fathima, the eldest daughter, was the second to succumb to mental illness, and her unhelpful label was manic depressive. Fathima was the closest among us siblings to the cultural roots of Sri Lanka and Malaysia, though she did not actually understand or know what that meant. She wore saris as a testament to some thread or idea of being Indian, professing her affinity and solidarity to her culture despite the fact that we rarely went to Sri Lankan functions. There were the one-off celebrations, but our daily lives were poles apart. She grew up with issues surrounding what was feminine and beautiful.

Fathima needed someone to talk to her about her issues. There had to be a special someone who had the time to listen, because the pills weren't working. Even her psychiatrist told Ammah dismissively "Mrs Shan, I do not have time for your daughter". No one could help her, and everyone walked and then looked the other way. It was hard for me to feel my sister's fear. I would be wide awake with a racing heart; intermittently, she'd emit whispering sighs, and her chest would move with each breath she took. I would never have thought breathing could be so loud. Fathima's fear was contagious, and I became nervous about an irrational fear.

At night-time, Fathima could not decide where she wanted to sleep. She would come and sleep with me, but this was scary too.

Fathima was the second child to have suffered fully the debilitating disease called "mental illness". She was sectioned in a mental hospital in Epsom and underwent ECG treatments, where the psychiatrists attempted to cure you with electric shocks to the brain. Fathima was always afraid, a fear that was crippling and debilitating. She could not remember to do mundane tasks like brushing her teeth, combing her hair, or washing. She wore the same sets of clothes, not caring about the latest fashion or her appearance. How could you deal with your issues when you are so heavily medicated?

The girls except for Hamza – Fathima; Aunty, Ammah's sister who was disabled; and I – all shared a room. Hamza had the smallest room in the house, the size of a storeroom or a prison cell, with a wardrobe outside in the corridor. This was the room that was used as the pokey kitchen for the tenants. Hamza decorated the walls with posters of Emilio Estevez and Rob Lowe, the latest American teen heartthrobs.

At this point, I thought Ammah should have to switch Gods or, at the very least, give up praying. Ammah was determined, and she did the best she could for her children in the only way she knew. Ammah went from church to church, from country to country on a pilgrimage, from one prayer meeting to another, from day vigils to night vigils. She was fasting and reciting litanies and one in particular "for the sake of his sorrowful passion have mercy on us and the whole world". Her knees must have been sore for all the kneeling and worshipping she did before God, pleading for her children's health. She would even have the parishioners around for prayer meetings at the house, in an attempt to cure all the ills in the family house.

Papa would ask, "Where are all your prayers going?"

To the outsider, we were the cursed family, deserving to be punished for something our ancestors had done. Ammah prayed for the family tree, attempting to cure or make recompense for the any misdemeanour of the forefathers. She did not want her children to pay penance on earth for their sins.

🦋 🦋 🦋

Ammah sent us three girls to Lourdes in France and asked her church friends, Patrick and Agnes, an elderly Irish couple devoted to each other and loyal to God, to look after us. They were the cutest elderly couple who complemented each other and competed to get to the pearly gates first. Hamza was a budding photographer and she created an album of the trip to Lourdes; in it, it appeared we were having way more fun than we did. No one would ever suspect we were on a religious retreat.

Patrick would say, "I did not see you girls at Mass." He tried continuously to get us to get with the spiritual program.

Hamza was a chip off the old man's block when it came to taking photos and had an acute acumen for storytelling with photography, which she shared with Papa. Both captured moments on camera. Papa would march the family to the local photo studio on his birthday. A present he allowed himself was a family photo. It was not necessarily a repeat occurrence every year, as with time, this indulgence too faded into obscurity. It was only fitting that she inherited all of Papa's collection of film slides.

🦋 🦋 🦋

After the suffering Ammah went through with Abijan being diagnosed with schizophrenia at age eighteen, it was as if God was playing a cruel joke, a sort of trick, when Fathima was diagnosed with depression. As a family, we had to deal with Fathima being ill. How could we help?

First, we needed help to understand what mental illness was, instead of buying into the claptrap that mental illness was a figment of one's imagination. Really, have you ever tried positive thinking and prayers when you have no control over a racing mind that never slept? Baloney!

Fathima did try to find her own self-expression, but it did not follow the norm and was not really accepted by her peers. Hamza, my friends and I were self-absorbed with our own issues of womanhood, boys, make-up, jobs, and nightclubs.

I was baffled. I could not determine what triggered Fathima to change from the bubbly personality she was to the troubled woman with mental illness. When she spiralled further down into her depression, I could not understand the reason for her decline. Fathima's selling points were those caterpillar eyebrows and her curly naturally wavy jet-black hair. She matched this with her mother's smile for everyone, along with a bubbly personality. She was not skilled in putting on the feminine package for the world stage. It was unfortunate that, when Fathima cut her hair short, just like Samson and Delilah, she lost her power and her confidence and doubted her looks. Fathima, pre-pills and pre-ECG, was the epitome of "black beauty" – raw and unrefined but natural. She was never going to be the cookie-cutter image of beauty, but was it fair for the world to demand that from anyone? Does confidence speak of beauty? And why could she not be happy? Fathima had always been connected to Ammah with an umbilical cord, attached more firmly now that she was ill.

The psychiatrists experimented with Fathima and tried various cocktails of pills. Fathima's jaw would lock, which made eating a horrendous task, and for the bystander, it might well have been a disturbing sight. She could not smile or chew her food because of the lockjaw, and her face froze as her skin pulled taut. There was no facial expression, no smile, just a vacant look and unblinking eyes. The side effects of these pills included hunger; she could eat at least three dinners, and her weight piled on.

For Ammah and the rest of the family, Fathima appeared possessed. Ammah was exasperated at the open blasphemy of a religious object when Fathima took the crucifix and hit the wall. Ammah sighed and was beside herself. There are many ways you can lose someone – not just by death; mental illness also parts you. As a family, we became estranged with Fatima, and she became this distant unfamiliar person. She would now shy away from the limelight, in much the same way as I would much later on in my life.

Ammah explained depression and mental illness as an evil curse – possession by an evil spirit. Spiritualists can be paid to do good deeds or bad. She blamed Fathima's and Abijan's illnesses on the cause of jealousy. Ammah was strongly rooted in culture and religion as it was her foundation of strength.

Ammah even went to a spiritualist and had the house exorcised. One of the spirits said. "I am glad to get out of this house; it is noisy and chaotic." The other spirit said, "I am sorry I caused so many problems."

I was glad that even the spirit was a witness to the chaotic shenanigans that went on in our red-bricked black-mortar house. I could not understand why anyone would ever be jealous of Ammah and her children. Ammah's children were neither rich nor smart nor good-looking. Neither did we move in the so-called elite circles. Soon I would understand that jealousy had many faces – that even the banal could trigger the nasty in a human being.

🦋 🦋 🦋

Fathima had been attempting to kill herself for a few years now and did not care about the spectators. It was a groundhog day, each day a repeat of yesterday. The family became desensitised, seeing her do the same thing every day, a few times a day. No one dared to think she would ever succeed. Self-strangulation with a cord or her bra was never going to work.

However, Fathima did succeed, and the restaurant owner of a famous small café found her. Ammah had been walking up and down the road asking people if they had seen her daughter. A policeman and a few people were gathered outside the restaurant. Ammah asked the policeman if it was her daughter.

That particular night, I had gone to visit my educated cousins, secretly desiring the polish of *a university* education. A sense of foreboding and unease overcame me that pushed me to call home. I held the receiver. Ammah said, "You'd better come home; she has gone."

Fathima had died, and I made the journey home alone, by bus.

At home, the family started calling family and friends to tell them that Fathima had died.

Papa and I went to the hospital to see if we could see the body. We were told that the body had been moved to the coroner's office and that a post-mortem was to be conducted.

The next few days were robotic. At the coroner's office, the family looked at Fathima's body through a glass window; only a white sheet covered her body, and she lay cold on a table in another room. The family just saw her face and were denied access. I knelt down and begged my sister to forgive me for not always being there for her and for running away.

I returned home that night, and when Papa opened the front door, Abijan ran out the house. We had just lost Fathima, and Abijan looked hell-bent on doing the same thing. Papa said, "Get him," with his usual poker face. But this time, his eyes were scared and his eyebrows closed; a frown appeared on his face, and his eyes lined in worry.

I chased after my brother as he ran into the road and nearly avoided being hit by a black taxi. I counselled him again and brought him home.

Before the body could be released for the funeral, there was an autopsy to determine the cause of death and an inquest after the funeral by way of an investigation. The autopsy was conducted, and it was determined that no foul play was at hand. She was gone in nineteen seconds, the time it took to end a life and to end her pain.

The inquest surrounding her death was conducted, and I accompanied Ammah and Papa to court. Papa and Ammah were quiet and said nothing. The judge said, "This is the only investigation that I conducted, where people are not blaming anyone for Fathima's death." I suspected at that time that inquests, by nature, laid blame at the feet of the root cause as to why a person turns up dead in a public place. The judge asked the psychiatrist, "Why, if the drugs were not working, did you not try something else instead of increasing the dosage, when it was clearly not working?"

I said nothing; I wished I could have said more – stood up for my parents who had lost their daughter. I stood silent, bowing down to my parent's authority half-expecting them to take action and not wanting to challenge Ammah and Papa's right to be silent. I believed that you had to take it all, not challenge the powers that be. I wished to be educated so that I would have the power to fight but, one way or another I was rendered powerless.

Ammah let things happen to her and was unable to fight – neither for herself nor for her children. She believed her own indoctrination that you only went to heaven if you were simple and accepted everything without complaining or rocking the boat. "What is the point of taking the matter further; no amount of money can bring her back," she determined in her grief. The judge ruled and the verdict given was "accidental death", and Ammah was blank.

I thought this was one kindness done by a stranger in power. He had the heart to overturn self-blame and recriminations and to ease Ammah's pain. The death certificate did not read "suicide".

Fathima's death scarred me beautifully. You had to value life; you had to do the best you could. You could never give up on anyone until they were gone. After Fathima's death, the family realised that neither pills nor "mind over matter" had worked.

Years later, I understood a play I had studied as a teenager in high school for my O Levels. I conducted my own social post-mortem and recollected *An Inspector Calls*. I understood the author's message that there is a chain of events in everyone's life, and we can only do our best to make life bearable and beautiful, if only for a moment. If, by our act, we can alter the fate of another positively, we can only try. Unfortunately the lesson in this play is that, even though we have this taste of a lesson, we have to sometimes relearn the value of life by having a full dose of proximity. Experiencing a thousand deaths has an effect, but unless you are affected directly, impacted by the deaths of those closest to you, a thousand deaths will always be a numbers game. I felt cheated by Fathima, guilty, and regretful. A chain reaction of events in her life had led to such an ending. I could not fathom whether a single action or a culmination of actions was to blame.

Again, I wondered – what causes success and failure in life? How does one become happy?

When the body was released from the coroner's, the family went to visit Fathima at the funeral parlour near our local church. Her face was bloated, slightly tilted down, and she felt cold to the touch, smooth like marble. Ammah took her gold earrings and replaced them with costume jewellery. I wanted to scream, *Let her have her earrings,* but had no voice and only looked on. This was my first experience of the death of someone close to me.

At the funeral parlour near the family's local church, we all went to choose the coffin. Ammah wanted one that was slightly expensive. Papa said, "She is my daughter. I will pay for the coffin."

Walking back from the funeral parlour on our street, Papa held Ammah's hand. This was a rare moment of emotional support that we children witnessed.

I had to find a way to fill the void left in Ammah's heart; I resented that she still missed her eldest daughter. Ammah secretly blamed Papa for not keeping a better watchful eye on Fathima the evening she went to the restaurant.

The local newspapers tried to talk to the family and got a few one-liners.

Some of Ammah's church friends came to give their condolences, and as Papa offered to make tea for them, one of Ammah's church friends said Papa was heartless. It was that same poker face that was misleading. He did feel.

I could never have closure, not even after the funeral. I could not understand why my sister had done what she'd done. I did, however, come to understand and realize that as siblings we were immature and unable to cope with her illness. It was Ammah who was the patient carer.

❦ ❦ ❦

Ammah bonded with the owners of the restaurant where Fathima was found. Nearly every Christmas, she would give them a card and a present. She would wave at them as she walked to church for the regular 9.30 a.m. Mass. They felt dreadful that such a thing had happened in their place. I wanted to go to the restaurant and see the place where my sister had died, except every time I came close, I saw their troubled gaze and turned away. I lost my courage. I wanted closure and wanted to feel Fathima's physical presence in a spiritual way.

I missed Fathima, especially when the phone calls from Ammah and the siblings were not so frequent from London and I was going through my own twisted journey in Canada. It was comforting to have an older sister, someone who loved and protected you. I looked back at a time when Fathima would make sure I ate my vegetables. With the birth order completely messed up, I now had to step up to the plate – be the eldest sister and look after the young ones.

I would make many "mistakes" in my support of my younger siblings, and they would come to resent and detest me for having made some of the decisions I made.

I tried to be like my mother – good, caring, and self-sacrificing. But really, did the apples fall too far from the tree? These apples, Hamza and I, were shaped differently. I was a "wannabe"; I wanted to be my mother but I wanted to be free like the mocking bird, so high in the trees that no one could touch me or torment my soul. I felt the chains of love that overlooked my sense of freedom, it was an internal conflict. I admired Hamza's ease that she fitted in her age that somehow, she was always in the right time frame, she made enjoying life effortless. Nobody, not one single child, ever wanted either Ammah's or Papa's life.

As a family, we each grieved on our own, and no one talked about the experience or how we felt; we all learned "doing it alone" as a way of copying, so as not to burden the other.

I wanted to bring life to the family, to bring hope of a new beginning. I had qualified as a hairdresser and was working in a salon, but I had to put aside foolish creative ideas and grab my own chance at life. I enrolled in a residential adult college for women and pursued a course, with the goal of going to university and becoming a professional. I wanted to be a lawyer, to be able to have the confidence to fight and be the voice in the courtroom, and to fight for the underdog. I wanted to lift the curse of the family and be successful and enrolled to study English at Lancaster University.

Papa came to visit me. I felt strangely proud of his visit, not at all embarrassed that he was there. When the students dashed into the communal kitchen to make dinner, I wonder what Papa thought about the food lockers with a padlock. He wanted to bathe in some glory that one of his children had made it to university. Both Papa and I wanted a taste of what all the fuss was about.

After I had completed my degree, he rang his friend in Singapore and said, "Idhaya got her degree."

🦋 🦋 🦋

After finishing my BA at Lancaster University, I enrolled at Exeter University to study law. A month into the course, I receive a phone call that my Uncle had passed away and six months later another call informing me that Papa was in hospital, and I made the journey home to see him. At Hammersmith Hospital, Papa was under the care of a team of nurses, doctors, and surgeons who were there to fight for him; they took it personally when someone died. I knew he had the best team to fight for his life.

Papa suffered several strokes and had to breathe through a respirator attached to his throat; he had plastic tubes and IV lines, and his breathing was laboured.

Papa was quiet about his ischemic heart disease, failing kidneys, and strokes, so when the surgeon met with the family and listed his health problems, the family was shocked and ignorant. We looked at each other vacantly and accusingly. *Did you know?* Papa never really had anyone to confide in about his illness. Truly, there was no one to listen to him, and I suspected he knew that if he attempted to try to talk about what was going on with him, there would only be more disappointment. He coped without people worrying and fussing around him.

Papa's younger brother from Singapore came to see him. Ammah and Uncle competed to find a cure for Papa. Uncle had a photo of Sai Baba under one side of his pillow, and Ammah had an image of

Jesus on the other side. Ammah was slightly flustered but they both respected each other, overcoming religious differences and uniting with the intention of Papa's health and recovery.

After the hospital visit, Uncle, Ammah, and I went home, and there we found the silly boy trying to hang himself with his belt. Uncle slapped him and said, "How dare you do this to your mother?"

I thought, *He sure picked his moment. Why now?*

I failed to understand the severity of mental illness that can strip you of your empathy and compassion. I could only see my mother's pain and thought rather foolishly that my brother was faking it or seeking attention. It is hard when you have someone trying to fight for life physically and someone in pain mentally is trying to end it all.

Having to deal with his guilt, regret, and recrimination as to why Papa was lying in the Intensive Care Unit was not something anyone considered into the equation.

Under the doctor's advice and reassurance that they were doing everything for Papa, I returned to Exeter again. I tried to focus and to catch up on my studies. It was just too important.

Two days later, I received another call from Hamza. "You'd better come home. Papa is going."

The train journey alone was filled with apprehension. I was going home to say goodbye for the final time. Papa's brother met me in London King's Cross station and said, "You have to accept this; this is part of life." At King's Cross station, the march of the ants continued— commuters, travellers on their own journeys, all unaware that my Papa was dying.

🦋 🦋 🦋

The life support machine was switched off. Ammah and the remaining four children gathered round Papa's bed. The nurse gave us a letter board and pen, and the hospital team moved back to give the family time and privacy to say goodbye. The flurry of activity and energy in the hospital seemed to have quieted down. This was not how it was to end; Papa was supposed to live.

I did not want to waste my time communicating with him; I was shocked and numb. I did not want to be robbed of the last moments, wasted by trying to say what should have been said a long time ago. I watched him die as he winked a last goodbye.

Balram said. "Papa, you go. I will look after the family."

I never even said "thank you". I stood still, tears falling down, never moving. I believed in miracles and expected them; my faith was that strong. I never gave up – not until it became clearly obvious that no miracle was going to happen and Papa was going. His toes were black due to the poor circulation, and he was having difficulty breathing. I started to sing the hymn "Do Not Be Afraid" so that Papa could die in peace. I knew that, if it meant the loss of his legs, Papa was going.

Papa died three days before his seventieth birthday, and we begged the hospital to keep him alive just so he could make it to his seventieth birthday. He was in the intensive care unit, the last stop, for three weeks. Now looking back, I saw that it was a selfish and childish request. From a smart-looking man who was proud of his appearance and ballroom dancing days, with his white suit and crocodile shoes, papa became the bald eagle and a slow walker. And finally, I lost him as he took his last breath and closed his eyes.

The calm and quiet flurry of activity and energy resumed in the hospital and the family was ushered out of the ward quickly when the flat line on the monitor came. The nurses took care of the dead and the near dying at the last stop ward.

Ammah was lost when Papa died. The entire family was lost. The head of the family had left us, and a new captain was at the helm, steering the ship through the crashing waves and stormy skies. Nobody can understand what goes on between a between husband and wife; Ammah was lost without Papa. She coped with everything with Papa at her side. They were the little and tall combination and pulled together, rowing the boat throughout the storms of Abijan's illness, Fathima's illness, and ultimately her death.

When Papa died, Ammah had a chance to hold her eldest daughter's ashes again, and she held Fathima's ashes tightly. Papa had just died. I remembered that moment, an eternal photo in one's memory – the bond of the mother and child, which I now knew was unconditional and surpassed all wrongs. This was not just Fathima's ashes – the remains of a body – it was all Ammah had of her daughter. Ammah smiled at me, and at that moment, I knew a mother's love. To watch your Ammah bury your sister teaches you the importance of a love of a mother for her child. It is true you can replace a man but not your child or your parents.

At home, I pieced together a story from Papa's death; there were bottles of pills and creams in his drawer. I opened his cupboard and found a few shirts and underwear in their plastic wallets, never used, never opened – presents people had given him. Papa lived a lie. You see, he was not a healthy man. To his children, he was old at sixty-nine, but the reality had only sunk in when he'd walked to Hammersmith Hospital because he was experiencing pains. Being tight with money, he didn't even spring it for a taxi to go to the hospital.

Papa was always careful about money, and to the family he seemed quite the stingy guy. As a teenager, in London I would hear how stingy the "Scot man" could be; as the saying went, he would refry a chip in the chip pan. I would later see the uselessness of stereotyping, but if the saying held any truth Papa could make a Scot's man look generous. He would never give Ammah extra money, even when people came for dinner. Ammah was given a housekeeping budget. She would ask the corner shop to let her have the chicken on loan until payday. The shopkeeper would be kind enough to do this. He was immigrant to England. He extended this courtesy to other customers. There was a certain helpfulness that went beyond race, religion, and culture. It was a bond that spanned the years. Perhaps an immigrants' experience was similar to that of Jesus when he went out into the wilderness. I thought that, if other people had such an experience, they would realize that they could find God, not in religion, but in those who helped them carry their crosses, rather than sit on them. We can broaden our scope of the meaning of "family" to include others.

Papa was good with some misplaced one-liners, such as, "I am your father and not your friend", which left everyone wondering what the context was. By the time Ammah confided in Papa about what was bothering us, Papa would always chip in, a month or two later, saying, "It's not the end of the world." It was his way of supporting us.

At Ammah's death, Balram, being the eldest son, would recall a number of one-liners he'd received from Papa. They would haunt him. Papa would speak to Balram outside the house at the black wrought iron gate, away from the family. They were bonding, and it was "men talk". Balram recalled that, in the fog of his grief that Papa had told him, "You can only help them when they fall" in reference Hamza and I. The best one-line Balram recalled was, "If a man gives you a watch, you are going to say, ah lovely watch and wear it with pride, showing it off, but if a man gives you a pile of shit, you are not going to carry it around."

I could not understand why Balram had issues with our father when he'd left him so many memories of a father and son. I had not had the privilege of communicating with my father, and I sought to understand my father through the many one-liners and stories told about him by family, friends, and my brother.

Balram was the proud owner of the biggest ego and, really, it ruled and ruined his life. His course of life was rough and controlled by himself. The river runs its course, over debris and stones, and the current in Balram's life was the river. A course set by nature or free will, the river and Balram allowed no external interference to steer him off course into a different direction. Balram was at the foot of the falls. Balram's life was now at the edge and soon to spiral uncontrollably down. Balram was the water that knew no control; the only thing that pulled him was his notion that money would give him respect. Nobody could tell him anything. He knew everything about everything. Balram, with his bald egg-shaped head could have been mistaken for an Ethiopian or a man from Somalia. His Arab friends described his face as a "money face".

Balram drowned in alcohol because his expectations of himself were somehow tied with money. He drank to forget his wasted youth, his failures, and his disappointment. The family waited for him to make millions. Balram did not like the man in the mirror. Papa said, "You can fool everyone but not the man in the mirror." This, along with other statements, would resonate at Ammah's death.

I had tried to say in hundreds of different ways "don't drink", but my brother liked his bottle and lived a life of denial. Papa used to say, "Money and education don't buy you respect." It was not sour grapes; I think there was something in this one-liner. No one respected Papa more for soldiering on with his health problems without telling anyone to spare us the pain. He did not burden us and gave us our shot at life.

Free will and being an adult meant I could not stop Balram from his slow suicide. I sought different combinations of phrases in the hope that there was one line, one phrase, one magic potion that would take away all his pain, and he would be on the road to recovery, a road of self-help. Balram wanted to give "big", "help", and be the "go-to" guy. The irony of life was he was unable to help himself. How do you get through a person in denial and chip away years of built up resentment, years of disappointment? There was no pill, just booze.

Balram being the eldest was the golden child with a carte blanche in his hand. Nobody dared judge him or question his actions, and slowly he struggled to keep Papa's house in memory of him and had to fight a court case when the family was stuck paying a hefty hospital bill for Ammah's brother who came to visit and accidentally set himself on fire. In many respects, his heart was golden, but he was a taker. Balram took advantage of everyone, unintentionally, relying on a promissory note from a distant rich man who played games with the poor hungry for wealth.

In the end, I resolved that I could not live his life and was only responsible for my own decisions. Did I have a right to kill a dream? We all have dreams; some just come with a heavier price tag.

The years rolled by and the family waited and waited for Balram to give big. I secretly cheered and held onto the hope that, one day, it would be him to give to Ammah and bring a smile that went straight to her eyes. I wished it would be him, not me. His eyes were sad and pained. The booze had marked him beyond recognition. I knew that it pained him to see me, as if it reminded him where he was in his life. I knew that it would hurt him, so I kept my contact and phone calls to a minimum. Seeing him hurt me too.

Being in a family was like playing on a hockey team. I felt the burden of Ammah's sadness; in my family, I navigated to score the goal for our team. Balram felt the burden of picking up the slack when I left for my shot at life. When my sister died, I went to university. When my father died, I married a Tamil Sri Lankan; a gift for the family was my marriage to a Sri Lankan. Happy times were ahead for all.

Unfortunately, I did not have time to grieve. I so aspired to be "normal" and desired a home life where cookies were baked and mothers and daughters were close. I wished for a family in which family dinners would revolve around discussion of world events, religion, and even philosophy. No one had time to ask about what was happening in the other person's life. I was fed up with constantly trying to give Abijan reasons why he should live and the drama of going in the ambulance again to get my brother's stomach pumped when he had swallowed a bottle of his own pills. "Think about Ammah and what you are doing to her," I would say. "She just wants you to have a good life. If you only thought of her pain and suffering, you would stop what you are doing." I was fed up to my back teeth of all the scaremongering.

Ah, to be normal and have people come and talk to you, rather than the isolation I felt as a family struggling to fit into the world, to find a niche, to find a worthy participating slot, and to stand and there and be counted.

Out of the Abyss:
A Ray of Hope

I was studying to be a lawyer at Exeter University when my father died in March 2000 and, out of nowhere, in April that same year, a proposal came by a phone call from overseas and later on a photograph of my intended husband. Ammah was excited; she told me that Papa had secretly been writing to my godmother Hannah in Malaysia, asking her if she knew anybody suitable for me to marry. I had no idea Papa was worried about such things. In the past, when Papa's relative from Sri Lanka sent a photo of a girl and asked if he could "find a suitable husband for the girl," Papa replied, "I can't get my own daughters married."

I was thirty-four years old, and the biological clock was ticking the usual tick-tock song; the intended bridegroom was also older. Being thirty-four, I was limited in my choices of Indian men, so I made do with what was available.

My friend Bethany, an English working-class lass with a heart of gold and a saviour of strays and waifs in the animal kingdom, was my companion on a quest for love. She would constantly set me up with blind dates, men who were either too short or too tall, foreigners who did not speak English, a stunt man/male stripper (he was a stuntman by day and a stripper by night), the butcher in Bermuda (assuring lamb chops and steak for Bethany), a hardnosed director, a handsome scientist. There was a Saudi Arabian Prince who turned out to be a chauffeur of mixed blood, Jordanian and Irish, living in Bethnal Green,

London. Bethany did not want me to waste my time. "You will never be this age again." Remembering Oscar Wilde's quote, "Youth is wasted on the young." I thought, *Oh how true!*

My family called and told me to look at the photograph. Hamza said, "You should come and look at him." Even Aunty Daisy said, "Idhaya, you should look at him; he is not bad, good-looking."

I saw the photo of a sophisticated and flashy man in his purple shirt, a poser for sure. He exuded confidence and had a sense of self-assuredness, and I would never have guessed that the world had not been good to him. I studied the photo. His eyes seemed angry, and he looked rigid, with a feigned relaxation. Even though his pose was relaxed, he appeared to be standing at attention. Still, I thought, *Not bad.* I was slightly worried about the prospect of being with a hard and angry man, but I put aside my doubts. I knew I could love the hardest of man.

First, the prospective in-laws, Mr and Mrs Devadas, came to visit. We were all seated in the living room. My future mother-in-law, Rebecca, was elegantly dressed in an off-white sari with a long string of beads round her neck. "I think this might work," she said. I did not know. She knew her son better than I did. "Go and get dolled up and get a professional photograph taken at the studio." She advised me.

He was a professional engineer. Papa would have been proud.

My future father-in-law, Indran, remained quietly on the peripheral radar, and his wife spoke for both of them.

Ammah would not leave her disabled sister in the dining room, as she was not ashamed of her sister. When the dreaded phone call had come to ask how Fathima had died, Ammah advised me, "You must tell the truth." My mother told me that I couldn't hide things and that my prospective husband deserved to know the truth. Ammah was straightforward in her beliefs, without any blurring of the grey. She would say, "Tell the truth and shame the devil" and "Truth shall set you free" – clichés, no doubt, but still, poignant.

I decided to give it shot, driven by a desire to please Papa on the other side, driven by some false notion that Papa from the heavens had some hand in this earthly arrangement. Really, how bad could it be? A sure win at the races – you meet; you get married; and then you have the white picket fence, 2.5 children, two cars, a single home, and tea with the neighbours. I rationalised that being of the same race and religion had to make a better base for the marriage than choosing someone from a different background. I'd had more than my fair share of blind dates and relationships with no-hopers.

On a wing and a prayer, I decided to give this a go. There were several email exchanges between my future husband and me, one in which he fancied himself as Don Quixote, a knight to the rescue, complete with cobwebs and rusty armour. In another email, he tagged a study on successful relationships. I felt strongly that arranged marriages would work. Love would blossom afterwards, like it had in my father and mother's marriage – the awe of climbing Mount Everest as each wedding anniversary passed was, no doubt, a worthy trophy. I could look forward to death as the only parting.

Soon, I was anticipating the arrival of my prospective suitor, Andrew. When Andrew came from Canada with a bunch of dying flowers and a box of Godiva chocolates, my inquisitive brothers looked on from the upstairs window. As he handed over the flowers and the wilting petals fell to the ground in the corridor, he looked quite perturbed. He confessed, rather embarrassingly, that he'd bought them from a nearby petrol station. His discomfort was noticeable on his face as we both looked down at the drooping bunch of flowers. I wore a dress but with the cardigan inside out. He was shocked to his core when my lipstick was on my teeth. I changed into my pants because I was more comfortable and thought I had lost the deal; he would not marry me now.

We went to the local pub and had dinner at a restaurant, and I told him the family's skeletons.

Balram scolded me, "You are washing dirty linen in public, and you sold the family short."

"Far from it," I said. "We were raised to be honest, if only to be fair to the other person."

I wished for an honest relationship, where my partner and I could be there for one another. Ammah felt that, because of the circumstances surrounding Fathima's life and death, I would never marry. Like Ammah, I was not ashamed of my sister.

Andrew, my prospective husband revealed that he dyed his hair and, due to a *motorcycle accident,* he did not like to wear shorts.

Andrew, the prospective husband, appeared scared, very scared. He had some inkling that this union might not work, because his family was a family who laughed like children and fought like children; yet, at the end of the day, they walked home as if nothing ever happened. There must have been a secret hidden reason for his apprehension. He made number of calls to his younger brother Stephen, the counsellor and guide in Canada, and was inevitably coached into submission.

Andrew and I had no real time to get to know each other, and everything about our courtship was abridged. He proposed after we both prayed in my local church, and I thought, rather naively, our union would be blessed forever.

He never once uttered, *I don't have the makings of a husband.* And I did not utter, *I need time to grieve and to finish my studies.*

My new mother-in-law did not want to wait because both bride and groom were older. I myself was not really in a good place at the time of my decision.

Andrew's well-known Sri Lankan saying was; "If you meet the mother on the street, you know what her daughter is going to look like." So off Sri-Lankan men would go to temples to look at their prospective mother-in-laws. Quite the comedy; if he believed this, then he should have left me in England. I too myself have heard of Tamil sayings and one in particular would mean so much "you tell a 1,000 lies to get a girl married" but how far is the manipulation of the truth acceptable?

Andrew's family came from Canada to England for the engagement. Johanna, his eldest sister, and her husband came with their children. I saw the way my future husband went to hold my handbag, and I glanced at his younger brother, Mark. At that time, I had a fleeting thought that, quite possibly, Andrew was a homosexual but brushed it aside. Mark stiffened, seeming to wonder if the new bride would guess the lie. I reasoned with and scolded myself. What utter nonsense; how absurd. *If he were gay why would he marry?* Surely, someone from my own race would not lie. It was probably because Mark's skin tone was lighter and because he was a pretty boy that I might have been inclined to believe that he would not be a participant in a family charade (which would reveal itself much later on). There were signs of incompatibility, but I brushed them aside and naively overlooked them.

The outward package looked reasonable, and no warning signs told me "If you enter into relationship with this, you may end up damaged, bruised, scarred, and cracked."

Andrew and I were registered at Brentford Town Hall in May. I was happy to have my cousin guide and convene the engagement. Kaneswari was a good-intentioned woman with caking decorating and bridal dressing skills. She was also apt at entertaining large crowds and made everything look easy. I had to marvel at the way she decorated cakes quickly and effortlessly. I trusted her guidance and knew instinctively my engagement would surpass my expectations and give the new in-laws a run for their money. Happily, I was rescued. My own family was clueless about the subtleties of welcoming the groom and family. We too were undercover, concealing the fact that we were not really know-it-all Tamils.

At the registry office, when the moment came to exchanging vows, Andrew seemed to stumble and could not say his name. He had a temporary dementia that lasted seventeen seconds, and his palms were sweaty. I looked at him, perplexed, and thought he would get there in the end. When questioned about his silence, he merely joked that he'd seen a pretty young girl pass by the window. Mark, his brother, said he was ready to wrestle him at the door should he wish to jilt the bride. I was not suspicious that his destiny was being played and mine dragged along. Where would it end? In those seventeen seconds, he gambled not only his future but mine too. He entered both of us into a contract, signing us up for a fate, the end of which neither one of us could see, though he must have had some inkling.

Bethany's mum Shirley came to the Brentford Registry Office after the ceremony to congratulate me. She piped, "Virginal, you look virginal." I could only cringe and hoped none of the family overheard the deliberate slip. I let out a giggle. I knew I was not a virgin; I had been with men before – errors of misjudgement or youth. I was not afraid because those without sin could cast the first stone. To delight in another's sin is useless and pointless. To put a hand around the shoulder of another and say, "I too have sinned" – that takes courage. The original meaning of sin is to *turn away*, and in many ways, we can *turn away*.

At the reception in England, when it came to toasting the crowd, my new husband said, "At last I have met the woman of my dreams." *Did he need to convince a crowd?* The aftermath of the engagement was filled with long laborious nights of partying, with the Tamils grabbing kitchen utensils, spoons, pots and pans, and Tupperware to make music. Out of their jacket pockets, they drew music sheets of the old Tamil Songs. Together, they would sing Tamil songs well into the night. A must was drinking hard liquor, Johnnie Walker Labels (Red and Black) whisky as another jolly beat.

My new husband was quite the showman; he seemed to enjoy singing, dancing, and storytelling. I looked on as the women served food for their husbands. They scooped rice and meat and vegetable curries on a plate and handed it to their husbands, and some even left a plate aside for when their husbands sobered up. It was at this point that I should have uttered, "I do not have the makings of a Sri Lankan wife."

I would cook, but the only person I served food was my aunt and those who were not able to serve themselves. Leaving a meal aside on the counter for the spouse after a drinking session seemed alien to me. I was never going to remember to do this.

My father-in-law, Indran, got drunk; he was happy about a marriage in the family. My mother-in-law was happy that she'd avoided the embarrassment of an unwed son, especially as everyone in the Sri Lankan community knew his secret; still he stayed in the shadows. Andrew wanted to be accepted by society as "normal, heterosexual" for himself and also to smooth the way for the family line, the next generation of children who had to wed in all the right circles.

I had my first Sri Lankan party, where Kool was served in England. Andrew told me to go upstairs and put my lipstick on before the guests arrived and I just followed his instruction. Kool turned out to the this great seafood soup with crab, fish, scallops, prawns and vegetables. All we lacked was the hot weather and a beach. The soup was quite a mouth-watering dish, with spices that threatened to make the tongue crack. Again, beer and Jack Daniels accompanied the food, a willing participant and an always-desired invitee. The labour-intensive cooking was a marathon, and the hostess would over-kill you with sugar, three lumps in coffee and tea, laddoo, burfee and cake. They believed extravagance in food was the right equation; cooking equalled love. Or was it working equalled love?

I rolled the dice of life, and being my father's daughter, I took a leap, a gamble; Canada and marriage to a Tamil was going to be win-win situation. I was, after all, leaving a chaotic and noisy home life – dysfunctional to the core, with my very own M25 motorway running through my house. Over the years, the house had seen a number of passers-by and many accidents on this hard and windy road.

I left England with well wishes and goodbye cards from friends, saying they hoped my new life in Canada was going to be everything I hoped for and that, if it wasn't, I could return home. My bid for escapism could, in turn, be seen as the hero's journey into the unknown – the idea of leaving and departing a life utterly wrecked by pain. My immigrant experience was totally different from Papa and Ammah's in that I weighed the pain I was leaving in exchange for a life. Papa and Ammah's immigrant experience was a uniting of a family and the success of the children which lured us to England for the grass that was greener.

Balram would say, "You were always running away from the problem." And though he didn't voice it, he viewed me as a deserter leaving him to cope with steering the ship and the family burdens. I was the coward who could not live my life but had to run to the other side of the world. "You have to stay and fight," Balram told me repeatedly.

Where did staying get him? Animals run away from sickness and death as part of nature's survival. I had to abandon the wounded for my shot at life. I knew that I was not alone in wanting to choose the joy of living. Even on our deathbed, we utter, "Give me time, more time." Was it so wrong for me to grab at life? I did not escape after all, Balram; the irony of my life was that I was supposed to go through the difficult emotional struggles fuelled by interactions with ill or abused members of another family – only this time, in the next chapter of my life (my marriage) the players were altogether different.

37

Canada, Here We Come!

I arrived in Toronto with twenty-seven members of my family, and it was quite the adventure. So many of my family and friends had come to celebrate and share in the happy time. There was warmth and compassion on this journey into the unknown, with a promise of happy ever after. Everyone boarded a flight from London Heathrow, England, and shared stories on the plane; a buzz of hope, a uniting of happier times to come vibrated in the air. From this moment on, I was a British Indian on a journey to Canada to be a South Indian Canadian.

At the new in-laws' home, a split-level bungalow backing onto a railway track, I was filled with dread. *Oh my God, what have I done?*

The split-level house with a basement was intimidating; there was enough space here to fit a small army. I felt intimidated and overpowered by a basement and a huge stone fireplace, not having owned one in England, and overpowered by the crowd of strangers all speaking Tamil. Perhaps, I was ill-at-ease because they all interacted so familiarily and I was now moving in mainstream Tamil society. They were all welcoming; they wanted their brother Andrew to be happy. And secretly, he wanted them to approve and be happy. Herein lie the disjoint.

Both sides of the family, Andrew's and mine, were here to have the church wedding – the proper religious celebration before God that made sure Andrew and I were man and wife. But in between all this, Balram had to cater to the elderly, the teenagers, and the small children.

Sightseeing was a must for everyone. It was a long way to go just to attend a wedding; we were, after all, in Canada.

We decided to go to the cinema and watch a movie. A passer-by told us the Cinema Theatre was two blocks down. A posse of Londoners took to the streets and quickly realised that we were the only ones walking and walking. Two blocks was quite the distance, not really round the corner. A weary group made it to the Cinema, and we all watched the latest chick flick.

I thought that Canadians were rich because the size of the houses and space was inconceivable. There was a bathroom on every floor, a powder room, a breakfast nook, a family room, a sitting room, and a dining room.

Ammah wanted me to meet Papa's long distant relatives living in Toronto because she was leaving her daughter in a faraway land with no guarantee that she would not need her Ammah. Going home to mother's, after a fight, was going to be an expensive business. The only repetitive assurance I received from my future mother-in-law was that she would love me like her own daughter. Years later, with the unravelling of the onion peel of half-truths, I would ponder: *Would she want the truth for her daughter or just the lie for her son?*

When I asked if two more families could be added to the invitation list, I was met with reluctance by my mother-in-law. "Oh, now I have to change the seating plans and everything. Why did you let me know at the last minute?"

I was not perceptive enough see that this was a clue – that, maybe, this was the first block of many to come. Seating arrangements for the reception were being arranged, and I had reached the point of no return. I could not allow any more doubt to ruminate in my mind; I had to let go of my doubts. I now entertained thoughts of newness – the adventure and the road ahead.

The Wedding Day

The wedding day was filled with promise. I was a new bride entering a lifetime commitment; to be with my one and only for the rest of my life was a prospect I looked forward to. I was appreciative of my good-intentioned cousin, Kaneshawari, who came again to navigate the cultural protocol and to dress me. I borrowed her jewels for the image of wealth and prosperity. Only Kaneshawari would be able to conduct an elaborate show of regal pageantry. She catered to the bridegroom's family.

The home of Kaneshawari's sister-in-law was the backdrop, and it was straight from a Bollywood movie. It was a huge house, even by Canadian standards. Kaneshawari welcomed the groom's family with her own unique flare. I followed the program as orchestrated by my eldest sister-in-law, Johanna, and it surpassed my expectations. I enjoyed the day, going with the flow and overcome with the blissfulness of the day. I wore a sari, and though I wanted a wedding dress, I thought, if the sari pleased Andrew, what harm was there? This was the inch I gave the family. I said my vows, and my uncle, Papa's younger brother, came to give me away. I had a white limousine and was driven by a chauffeur to the church. At Mass, there was the usual readings, gifts of offertory, and the exchange of wedding rings. There was the *thaali* (the gold necklace), which Andrew tied around my neck. Now, I was given away to him. This exchange was ritualistic and symbolic of the Hindu tradition. This was a merging or a sharing of culture and the catholic religion.

The wedding reception was again fun. The centrepiece and arrangements were amazing, and I was garlanded with a beautiful string of white flowers, which felt heavy to wear. The cake boxes were made in the shape of a butterfly in a brassy gold colour.

I was escorted to another room to change from the bridal wedding sari to the Koorai sari. *Koorai Pudavai* is a traditional sari, measuring nine years, and it turned out to be a gift from the groom's family to the bride. My Koorai sari was the same brick red as my Papa's house but had gold threading weaved into the material. The pleats fell straight and were centred against my body. I had to walk straight so that the pleats did not shift off-centre. Then there was the extra portion of the sari hanging down over the left shoulder. I would really struggle with draping the sari, having the right number of pleats and measuring the folds. I knew that walking in the sari while pulling off the elegance of a peacock required the right balance. Everyone was watching the head table, where Andrew and I were seated with the rest of the bridal party. I looked at the sea of unknown faces, the flowers, the dresses, and the smartly dressed men.

The toastmaster, Stephen, the comedian in the family, with his skinny latte complexion, could well be described as a shorter version of Elvis, a Mafioso type. As the younger brother, he would counsel Andrew throughout and acted as a mediator for both the family and Andrew. He was in his element, ensuring that everyone kept to the program. On the sidelines, my own brother Abijan was restless and refrained from making a scene. I only hoped, he would not take off his shirt and reveal the tiger on his back.

Andrew and I took turns to thank everyone for coming and participating in the happy event. Then we danced as newlyweds to Etta James's "At Last".

❦ ❦ ❦

Back at the family home, the split-level bungalow, my mother-in-law wanted to make breakfast, but my new husband stepped in. He wanted to take care of me – to make me breakfast, eggs, bacon, and toast. He was there pleasing everyone, but I just wanted to get him on my own, to have the time with him to properly get to know him.

I felt displaced; the formalities were over the top, the protocol stifling. I was afraid; I was not really sure how it would all pan out. I was dazed and overcome with stage fright. I was a home bird. I was not really "English" and not really "Sri Lankan". Yet I lived this in-between life and tried to straddle two cultures I did not fully understand. The day arrived when the understudy, unprepared, who did not know her lines or her new character, was pushed into a performance of her life. I hugged my family at the Toronto Airport and did not even shed a tear; we were all dry-eyed. All I knew was that my old way of life was now past and my family was returning to England. Slowly but surely, I would acclimatise to my new way of life.

# A New Beginning

The car ride from Toronto to Quebec was a long one, and I was filled with eagerness as I considered where I was to live and whether it would surpass my expectation. What was the place going to be like? I was blown over by the vastness, half expecting Quebec to be like the pages of the travel brochure on Vancouver that I'd seen a few years back. I passed through Ottawa and there were rows and rows of houses being built, single homes, mixed with townhouses and apartments. For the residents it was like living in a construction war zone as debris, dust and rubble entered their homes and they were woken up by the noise the heavy machines. As I approached Quebec, I thought I was definitely going to get lost – all that space and hardly any shops within walking distance; no tree or landmark stood out as a milestone. I would quickly learn how to get about by bus, walking in the soft snow in temperatures as low as -20 or even -40 degrees with wind chill – nature's way of giving me a facelift, pulling my skin taut; it was a deep freeze treatment for a timeless aging.

My mother-in-law came to spend a few weeks with the newlyweds, to make sure her new daughter-in-law did not miss her family too much. Ours was an easy relationship in the beginning. As a new bride, I wanted to please my mother-in-law. As the years progressed, we would become more like two women sharing than a new daughter-in-law trying to please her mother-in-law. We shared our loneliness and unhappiness, a bond that strangely crossed the generation gap. My mother-in-law was proud of me; she knew instinctively that I could handle life with her overwrought son. We got along famously, like a house on fire. She would teach how to make all Sri Lankan rolls, the fish buns and *murruku*, chippy, and *appam*. I would do all that she required with no questions asked. In those early days, she would constantly send me to the shops to buy the necessary kitchen utensils that she needed for her recipes. I was a willing skivvy.

Over the years, we would form a close bond and made a wicked combination, a mother-in-law and daughter-in-law relationship that would be supportive – a relationship that was the envy of many. Still with each year that passed, it became hard to look back at the relationship in the same way.

I would never have expected our relationship to sour and that her survival and unhappiness was the reason for her manipulation and secrecy. Years later, I would learn of the deception and I could not see past the lies and deception to ever believe she loved me.

If there was one favourable quality I did learn from my mother-in-law, it was not to waste a gift, to use your talent. I did not realise what my gift was but discovered writing, quite by accident, and though I could not fight in the courtroom as a lawyer, I had the pen to be the voice for those silenced. This time, I had the pen to reach out to people to let them know that they are not alone. I knew that, to respect a life lived is to remember something life changing.

Over the years, my in-laws realised they could not make a silk purse of a sow's ear. But, for me, all I would endure would be worth it, as I would learn the value of a gift and of using it as a service and I reconnected with my dream, my purpose.

Time, as I knew, would heal wounds but time was slow in passing and so, of course, I had to be patient with my healing at times I wonder if I ever would grasp that healing would eventually come to be. In the background of my relationship with my mother-in-law, Andrew and I became more and more silent with each other. It was as if he believed my relationship with his mother would compensate for any lack in our relationship. If his mother was happy, he was happy. He did not ask if I was happy, It was an ordained Tamil male privilege.

Neither of my parents-in-law was dwindling with old age; rather, they celebrated their milestones and their children's accomplishments, and given their humble beginnings as a married couple, they had every right to be proud. My mother-in-law was the archetypical mythological figure Draupadi, a feminist and traditional, a contradiction for sure, and I pondered this dichotomy. My mother-in-law too must have struggled with this contradiction, being loyal to tradition, culture, and religion but yet with a spirit of fire in her and, strangely, fragility. She would study all the medicinal properties of food and was an advocate of "heal thy self" with food for whatever your ailment.

My parents-in-law were both culturally and religiously bound, and only death parted them. Their backgrounds were very different; she was rich, and he was poor. In many respects, his wife's many talents overshadowed Indran, and he stood in the shadows while she ran the show. He fostered a spirit of competition in his children that was negative and destructive. Only the bloodline seemed to understand its value and could navigate without drawing blood.

My mother-in-law was one of the parishioners of the Little Infant Jesus Church and a reasonably well-to-do woman, endowed with many talents but none so telling as Mother Superior. In the community, everyone knew her. She was well-known in the community for her polished talents – cooking, sewing, and teaching. She swallowed a cocktail of vitamins to enhance the liver, the kidney, the heart, the mind, the eyes, the bones, and the skin. You cannot control the time of death; that belongs to God. Living can be as burdensome as the curses of men, but that curses, born out of envy, jealousy, and malicious intent are merely arrows of blessings, the merit of which is overseen by God.

A tally of her mother-in-law's good deeds was surely kept in heaven above, but none was more worthy than her inclusion of Celine, her husband's child, as her own. Away from the gaze of society and community, the heavens smiled because none but God knew the selfless giving it took to embrace another that which was not her own. To many, this inclusion was a misguided and foolish mistake, but my mother-in-law's inclusion of Celine created a family of God. She need not have worried about the judgment of community or society because, in the end, everything that happens is between "I and God" and not between "I and you". The "I and God" only steered the "I and you". All of God's

45

children must be held accountable to the same universal rule – the karmic rule of reciprocity.

But I would not learn of this situation until much later. And when I did, unfortunately, the family would cloud it with so many secrets and half-truths – involving my own husband and son – that getting to the bottom of it would nearly be my undoing.

In my first year of Christmas in Canada, I received cards, which were tongue in cheek. "I bet you are going to have a white one." Snow, my friends and family back home assumed, would be assured for Christmas. My first Christmas in Canada was quite the experience, and my New Year was a first Tamil New Year. I was again witnessing culture unfolding, the traditional Kai-vishesham, where the family members went around giving everyone money, loonies, and toonies. If you were lucky, you even received the big notes ($10, even $20 dollar using coming from Mark), but it was definitely not a "get rich" system you could rely upon. It was the Tamil tradition of wishing wealth for the New Year, and you were supposed to keep the money until the next New Year. Kai-vishesham seemed fun. I found it tempting to spend the money hidden on the top shelf under some shirts and cardigans in my bedroom wardrobe. I restrained myself and let the money sit there all year, so not to potentially jinx my luck. I needed my luck.

Every year the traditional sweets were made. Broavi, the hard marbled biscuit, could definitely crack a few teeth; I wondered how this treat had ever earned a repeat occurrence; or maybe it was there to be a jawbreaker for the undesired invitee. *Payasam* and *pongal* were sometimes made and sometimes left off the menu. Murukku, chippy and date cake, along with semolina cake and other extras were served. We all wore our new fancy outfits, which we'd bought for the occasion, and found out who our secret Santas were and worried about whether whoever we'd been secret Santa for liked our present. For two years running, Andrew had pulled out Dolly's name. He was filled with dread because whatever he bought Dolly, Stephen's wife, she was sure not to like it. Mark, his younger brother, offered to switch names, and that Christmas, Dolly did not mind the present. It was always quite a stressful operation, and with a few swaps here and there, everyone was happy. It was altogether a different kind of Christmas and New Year told in a different way. This was culture at its best, celebrating the coming together of loved ones – but sometimes I wondered if they were really loved ones congregated as much as obligatory invitees.

Soon, a few years later, Andrew would be working through Christmas, and I would spend the time with the family. The family was left to take care of me while he roamed free. I felt lonely the first few years. I felt his distance. Left to my own devices, I attempted to do everything on my own. I walked on the moist, slushy snow to Loblaws, but my runners did not do so well over the snowbank. The mighty machines had pushed aside the mountain of snow. I was literally forced to abandon the idea and paid attention to the television channels devoted to the weather.

The next time I went to Loblaws, I was surprised how helpful the employees were in serving customers. They were polite and courteous. Amazing! They actually took me to the aisle where the flour was kept, and I was impressed at how many types of flour and other baking ingredients were on the shelves. *Homemaker* had a different meaning in Canada, judging by the goods in the stores. I walked home, the tomatoes in my bags rolled out onto the road, and the bus driver thought I was crazy – join the rest of the world! I grabbed the bull by the horns and lived my life, come what may.

I told Andrew that I had an affair with a married man before my marriage to him; I wanted him to see that I was not this good girl, and just maybe he would make love to me more. I recollected early on in our relationship when my sister-in-law invited us to dinner and we were late; it was assumed that we, newlyweds, were having sex, and this was not the case. Sharing my past relationship with Andrew had the reverse effect, and the family knew about my mistake in my youth.

The days were short in wintertime, and Andrew and I became hermits, going out only for a couple of evenings in a week with his friends. It was dark going to work, dark when I came home. I had to dress for comfort, no high heels in the snow and no short skirts. Yet I was stunned to see the teenagers out in T-shirts and pyjamas in the cold weather, their challenging spirit defying winter and temperatures of -15.

I wore a parka and boots and, later on, bought snow pants that made walking in the snow all the more enjoyable. I did not have to worry about the salt on my dress pants when I went into the office. Andrew treated me like a child, wiping away the salt from my shoes and my pants.

We had a beat-up green Camry without any heat, and whenever I forgot my lunch, Andrew would drive to my office and give it to me.

I quickly made friends with another immigrant, Nasreen, in the apartment block, who would help me cook and advise me that I should always look good before Andrew came home. Looking good did not really help. I felt isolated, away from everyone I had known all my life. I missed the sense of ease you feel when you know a person, when you've shared all the storms, your fears, your doubts, and your aspirations. I had friends who were as comfortable as a pair of old shoes, ones who never abandoned you.

My eldest sister-in-law, Johanna, and others would take me to see the highlights of Canada, the Tulip Festival, and the fireworks for Canada Day, and the sculptures on offer at Winterlude. In Johanna, I saw a poet's eye – the ability to find the highlights in nature. I would take my friends around the usual tourist attractions. The second time Gillian came for a holiday she experienced her first winter blizzard and we drove and missed the exit for Buffolo. When Bethany came, she experienced Canadian wildlife by the unwelcoming presence of black flies and mosquitos, and I laughed when she spoke of half expecting to see a black bear but was worried about the West Nile.

It was my excuse too, to discover Canada and Quebec. I felt quite proud that I could spout out the various highlights in nature, such as the changing colours of the leaves, reds, oranges, yellows, browns, and deep purples. It was not the changing of the guards that spoke of Canada but nature, the pockets of streams, lakes, and waterfalls just a fifteen-minute drive away. It was extraordinary how the sun blazed upon the snow in minus temperatures, an oxymoron and a conundrum; I'd feel the coldness in my bones and the moisture in my boots and, yet, a gentle warm kiss from the sun. I was fragile and strong and yet comforted. My life swung in a pendulum from the storm to the calm.

These were the extremes in life for me – the rest before the work, the fight before the peace.

❧ ❧ ❧

A few years later, I learnt to drive, with the instruction of the driving school and Andrew. Well, Andrew's formula-one driving technique was not to be imitated; my pace was cautious and slower. After a couple of attempts in Canada, I finally passed. I had my first accident the same year I passed my driving test; it was a bumper-to-bumper accident. I was remembering Andrew's instruction that, *when you pass a car on the right, you have to speed up and get back into the lane quickly.* I hit the gas and quickly tried to change lanes, and the traffic lights changed to red. I was shocked when the safety bag exploded and the right side of the car crunched. The ambulance and police quickly came to the scene. I turned around to assess the accident scene and knew instinctively that the car was "beyond repair", our lovely green Camry demolished. I was pregnant with Kumar. I hit one lady from behind, and she in turn hit another lady who was also pregnant. It was now the pregnant convoy.

Driving gave me independence, but even with the great open space on the roads, I still managed to hog the road. I was honked at, sworn at, and hollered at to stay in my own lane. With each year, I got better and better at driving – more confident and comfortable. GPS was a helpful technical aid that nudged my adventurous and independent spirit.

Once, driving in a white-out, I prayed, *Oh my God, oh my God, don't let me die*, and, with my driving skills, *Don't let me kill anyone on the road.* I clutched the steering wheel and followed the red eyes ahead, keeping my car on the black tracks of the road. My car crawled slowly ahead. At some point, the journey was too frightful, and so I parked and waited for the snow to subside.

❧ ❧ ❧

I made friends on the bus, in Pizza Pizza, in the apartment block, at the gym, and in the park opposite my house. Soon, I would go to my new friends' houses and sit around their breakfast nook tables, and it was *The*

View, two emotionally unhappily married women, one divorcee, one widow, and an unworldly youngster. Slowly but surely, I built a support system. On those early immigrant days, the hot spots were walking around IKEA and having coffee and cake in Chapters; this non-daring group dared not venture too far.

Without my family and longstanding friends, I would find friends in strangers; one in particular who I helped would in turn help me. A Muslim and a Christian found God in each other. The grey areas of "helping" become blurred.

My own immigrant experience into Canada was altogether a different one from Ammah's into England. The immigrant experience was a peculiar experience, because, in isolation away from my family, I found a new family, and they were my Muslim, Hindu, Buddhist, and white sisters. In isolation, I was to question the stereotypes on which I based my knowledge and understanding of human beings.

I started to try to become a fully-fledged Sri Lankan. I bought the drumsticks, the idli mix, and the pots and pans to boot. I recalled making a drumstick curry for my sister-in-law Jessie's mother but omitted skinning the vegetable. I tried to make idli, and the mixture bubbled over in the pan and became porridge. I learnt how to make murrukku, Chinese rolls, and chippy but hardly practiced this. The steamed pittu could be cooked in a number of ways, and Jessie had the idea of using two cups rice flour and one cup plain flour in a baked version of the dish. The smell of the steamed coconut and flour was an aroma of Sri Lankan cooking, an incense that wafted in the room. I joined a sewing class and a cookery class and watched Hindi movies.

I remembered how my Ammah would make parata and murukku for the family dinner when we were younger, and this brought about great laughter. "For all you know, she still does," was piped from back of the van. What the in-laws had heard was *pārata piratamarukku*, which was literally translated as "someone who was farting". I was now trying to speak Tamil but this time I had an English accent, and it was clearly creating confusion and hysteria. I now had an accent of a different kind. My Tamil was broken. I could understand the spoken word but had difficulty speaking. Well at least Ammah had made both admirably.

The parties, dances, and picnics were an all-year event. At one Sri Lankan picnic with the family, I actually made a tasty banana chocolate chip cake, and everyone enjoyed eating it. When Patrick, my eldest brother-in-law, who was the firstborn golden child and a preacher, came for the last slice, I guarded the last slab of cake for Andrew. When I made something tasty, it was worth keeping for sure. I knew that repeating the success might be near impossible.

I wanted my isolation, wanted the mixed bag of people I'd grown up with. My new family knew how to appreciate living the good life, and I quickly realised I had to have a strong dose of thick coffee so that I could go the distance with the all-nighters. I began to understand that Sri Lankans were night owls. They would cook late, host guests starting at around 8.00 or 9.00 p.m., and we would eat and drink steadily well into the wee hours of the morning. The sleep routine was upside down, and my in-laws came alive, laughing heartily as more guests arrived.

Andrew: The Odd Duck Husband

*A*ndrew's eyes, as well as his demeanour, gave the sense of an everlasting wondering youth, an unfilled youth, perhaps a lost youth; his eyes were also coloured yellow with diabetes. He was five foot nine, slimly built, and had a mocha complexion, though some might argue he was a shade closer to the dark chocolate. He had the trademark Bollywood movie star Tamil moustache of a forever macho guy varying it only with a chin beard. His eyes wore many shades of anger and admiration. In the mirror, he would admire his reflection as he cupped the growth on his chin and trimmed his moustache. He looked younger than his years, but diabetes was attacking his system, and he was losing weight fast. Still, he maintained his macho image and continued to smoke and drink with his friends. His walk had a certain bounce and energy in the heels of his shoes, a basketball player's walk or Michael Jackson's moonwalk.

The early days of marriage were uneventful. Andrew was proud of me and introduced me to all his friends as "my wife, my wife", never using my name. I felt in some way objectified. At first, he seemed to like my naivety and inability to discern between a diamond and a zirconia. I, being educated and raised in England, was perhaps a novelty. I wasn't a threat because I wasn't a true-blue Sri Lankan. He would never let anyone put me down. He allowed no one to get away with a smart negative remark made against me. He was glowing over his new wife. I was never sure why he decided upon marrying me. Was it having a wife that made him feel *normal* or was there something particular in me that made him feel included? Either way, he finally had a prop in life that could help him be included as "normal" – whatever normal means.

Andrew took pride in my mistakes, as it permitted him avenues to tell stories. This was Andrew's striking crowning glory; he could command an audience with his narrative, using showman's tactics. He was a performer of the oral narrative, as he dared to say and do what others only thought. Harmlessly, he started to use my housekeeping errors as storytelling material – the first being how I'd put his favourite silk tie in the washing machine and it had shrivelled to a lesser thing and no amount of ironing had been able to restore it to its former glory. Next, there was the dressy white shirt, which I'd mixed with the colours. Needless to say, it was not a white shirt when I'd taken it out of the washing machine. I'd silently discarded it in the trash. Then there was the hot iron that had fallen to the ground and burnt a hole in the carpet and had become the talk at work, as all wondered about how one could ever doing such a thing, even as an accident.

Andrew was astounded that women actually farted. Nothing was safe between husband and wife. I picked my nose, and he told his family. I left sanitary towels on the bathroom floor; he told the family. I, too, could see the comedy of a number of things that I did wrong. With the years, this somehow slipped into finding fault, which made the comedy not so funny. I would be shocked when Andrew would look at me disdainfully whenever I misplaced my keys or left the keys in the door.

Once, my sister-in-law Dolly, Stephen's wife, was looking for her keys and I thought, *Here is another one.* The entire family hunted for the missing key. Patrick, Andrew's eldest brother, the golden child, went out into the night with a flashlight. I looked at Dolly in awe and then thought I'd better make sure I had my keys. I searched in my pockets and found that I had two sets of keys and that I had accidentally taken Dolly's keys. Andrew's gaze was intense and dumbfounded. He was astounded at my scattered mind and my forgetfulness.

Andrew was a controller, but maybe, deep down, he needed to control things because there were times that he lacked control. He calculated the number of ways that things could go wrong. He was always anticipating the worst-case scenario, which made his control seem negative and destructive. I would pack my son's lunch, but he would repack it; I would pack my own suitcase, but he would repack it with clothes he had chosen. I wore a dress, and he would redress me with clothes he had chosen.

He was the overseer, who watched how I cut the vegetables and acted like a supervisor. He stood by to instruct. I should use two knives, two cutting boards, one for vegetables, and one for meat. Invariably, he did not like the way I cut the meat; it had to be sliced against the grain. I did not care how onions were cut, but there was a certain way onions had to be cut. Cooking without the exhaust was a no-no, but in my forgetfulness and stress about pleasing, I would always forget to turn on the exhaust whenever I used the stove. He would tell me how to iron clothes, how to mop the floor, and what type of mop to use. Needless to say, I in my rush and panic to get everything ready, grew faster and faster at cutting the meat and vegetables, cooking, and cleaning the house.

Andrew competed with me in the kitchen; he was the chef and I the sous-chef. If I added more salt or curry powder to his cooking, he would snarl and appear ready to pounce for what he considered a deliberate act of "curry sabotage". Our roles were messed up. He loved being in the kitchen and hated the gardening. Whenever I cooked a delicious meal, Andrew would always find fault and would fix it to his liking. Personal taste meant that he had a right to choose what he put in his stomach.

I grew tired of doing everything for him. To have someone constantly tell you where you were going wrong and constantly watching you was exasperating. His desire for control was deeply rooted in his past. Finally, I resolved to cook for myself and leave him to fend for himself. He was, after all, a great chef, with an uppercase *C*.

I did acknowledge that his meals were tasty, though cholesterol rich; they went straight to the heart and blocked the arteries for sure. He would cook and dish the food on a plate and serve it to me. He made sure I ate well, but somehow, after the years of being worn down, cooking did not equal love. Andrew was half a controller and half a pleaser. I suspected this created his angst.

I could not relax; I was caught in Andrew's timeline, which was fast and furious. I had to march to his drumbeat. One evening, I was cooking Andrew a meal, but he arrived early. An onion peel was out on the kitchen counter, and he was upset that I had not finished cooking and the place was not clean. After his display of anger – during which he growled, "How can you let someone in the place when it is a mess?" – I would always chase my friends out of the apartment before Andrew came home.

Andrew's presence in the room would automatically straighten my back, and I would take the broom and start sweeping the floor. I knew that if Andrew knew my friends had been there, he would grumble and criticise me for having people around when the place was messy. I would scan the room, and to my not-so-keen eye, everything would appear to be in order – until Andrew came home. I would mop the floor, but he would say, "What are you doing? There is candle wax on the floor. You just put hot water on the floor, and you are spreading the wax around." I would get up and change the mop. Even when my friend came and she neglected to use a spoon but just tilted the jar of coffee into the cup, he would say "What is wrong with you? Can't you use a spoon?"

I was never going to be in a win-win situation, because Andrew was always there to expound on how I'd neglected to do something or how I should do something differently. The performance criteria were shifting and whimsical.

He would always use his ritualistic "show-and-tell" strategy as a form of control, a manipulative tactic to destabilise and make me believe that I was "not good enough" and "incapable". You see, Andrew and his family were just good at *everything*. He tried to manipulate emotionally, knowing my weaknesses all too well.

Andrew was fiercely competitive with his brothers. I was average-looking, but Andrew wanted to make me extraordinary so that he could push me "*out there*" on the centre stage, and while bragging about my talents, he could appear superior to his brothers.

Andrew and I were the odd couple, mismatched in every way; he was a boaster, and I a wallflower, seeking to camouflage my presence into the background. The bragging didn't stop and, in fact, made things worse for me, and the sisters-in-law were jealous of me. Their own husbands were not so vocal about their many talents. They were unnoticed and unappreciated. I sought to camouflage my presence into that awful patterned cushion on the sofa, rather than be pushed into centre stage. I wanted to participate, rather than be a wallflower but was too concerned about what my in-laws all thought of me. There were too many passing remarks over the years that made me doubt myself. Andrew wanted his brothers to feel that he had the best wife, but not because he was thinking of me. He needed to prime his peacock feathers for the front. I was becoming immune and desensitised to his flattery because it was reserved for only when there was an audience, the obligatory card and flowers on special occasions, and an embellished line. He was manipulating me emotionally into believing that he loved me.

Andrew desired never to be alone with me. He would leave me at Stephen's place for a week. After one camping trip with the boys, when he returned, I went to the front door eagerly, hoping to see a happy and excited face. Instead, he was angry and stressed, and I was left behind because he needed extra time; I was passed from one house to the other. Though the clues added up to one clear picture – that Andrew didn't want a relationship with me – I somehow didn't see them. I just wasn't looking for the clues.

A number of things didn't make sense to me, and they stood out like sore thumbs. Firstly, why was Andrew trying so hard in so many ways to demand respect? Why should a grown middle-aged man need the applause of an audience?

Secondly, it had always baffled me how Andrew could endure nastiness; I would later reflect that, perhaps, this ability had to do with the nastiness I witnessed not being the nastiest of human behavior that he had endured in his life.

My own family had not been that welcoming to him, and though this upset me, he was not upset. Or maybe the frosty reception was the excuse he needed to keep his distance. No one, in the beginning of our relationship, wanted to talk to him because he was such a know-it-all.

Later, there were the usual fights. In the end, I would call him a "homo" after he'd continue to call me "crazy". But I knew, because of the type of anger I had lived with, that his rage and outbursts were brought on by something else, something hidden deeply in his past.

Thirdly, why was Andrew always ready to do battle at parties, even with people who meant him no offence or harm? He was always breathing fire, laughing at first, and then, like a volcano, erupting at odd moments and in strange places. There had to be more to explain that type of anger that I had to live with.

In Name Only:
A Peculiar Tamil Wife

I n the beginning, the family would dress me and buy my saris; they would seem to help me choose, but really, they manipulated my choice of saris, almost as if they were the "in-the-know" fashionistas. I would not know my Kanchipuram sari from the Pashmina. The pallu was the most decorative piece of material of the sari; motifs were taken from the usual mythological symbols of the lotus, peacocks, and butterflies. My mother-in-law often used these motifs, hand painting them onto saris and ties and giving them to her sons and daughters as gifts.

The Brahmins had their own way of tying the sari, as did the people from Kerala. The underskirt, the *powada*, had to be the correct shade or hue so that it would not be seen when draping the sari, and I would have to follow the guidance of the sisters-in-law because I would not have selected the exact right tone. Whenever there was a party in Toronto and I was required to bring my saris, I would invariably forget my *powada* and ask Andrew, "Have you seen my power-there?" I was not pronouncing the word correctly and he was clueless, and again I would try, "Have you seen my power-there – you know, my underskirt?" Ah … finally he understood.

I would rather wear a salwar kameez – a trouser and top ensemble; it was less elaborate, but it sure saved a heap of time when getting ready for parties. The in-laws were always fashionably late, in time for dinner.

I was again clueless. I went with the flow because I had little know-how when it came to Sri Lankan culture. I was constantly under the watchful gaze of Andrew, the fashion and appearance police. Johanna, my eldest sister-in-law, was called upon on numerous occasions, along with the other sisters-in-law, to tie my sari.

The comedy of errors in the grooming department was always a source of stress. At one Sri Lankan function, my sister-in-law, Jessie, had to pull me aside and tell me that my sari was inside out. I was discretely led to the ladies washroom, where my sister-in-law reversed the sari. Being transformed into a cookie-cutter Sri Lankan Stepford wife was not only stressful but also soulless.

I recalled a co-worker, Judith, walking into my office, accompanied by a friend. "Can you tie my friend's sari?" Judith asked. "She's doing a parody of the lady in a sari who gatecrashed the White House for a dinner function."

I was taken aback and surprised to learn that no dress rehearsal had been scheduled for Judith's friend's performance. I admitted that, even though I wore saris at functions, I never really properly tied one proficiently enough to do it for another person. It was quite a stressful operation in the ladies' washroom. This whip of a girl was a size two, and the sari she was wearing had so much material. Two attempts later with the help of Judith, I pinned her so at least she was secure and sent her to her social event.

My style was casual chic; I wore little or no make-up and was comfortable in slacks and a T-shirt. I could get myself dressed into the polished and elegant style for a special occasion but not for an everyday walk to Walmart. It was never going to happen. I would always get into a tizzy and panic; my lipstick would be smudged; and my toenails were not always painted or, if anything, chipped. The tip-top grooming went as far as having bras pinned so that they didn't show through transparent blouses.

The in-laws still wanted the transformation for the public stage. Andrew wanted the transformation for his own reasons; a glamour puss would leave the world thinking he was the doting husband, and no one would question his sexuality. The extras invited to the party would all believe the charade of a happily married couple. He was so convincing that even I believed the charade of a happily married couple.

I brought over some jewellery that Ammah had given me. I guess the expectation was that you wore jewellery because a girl without jewellery was a poor girl. Whenever I wore my gold earrings, I would sleep with them in my ears, and by the morning, they would be bent. I probably had a collection of one pair of earrings, and only one of the pair.

My in-laws did not want a Tamil village girl from London, but I was a Londoner, a free bird, and a coconut. However, at times, when I carried three shopping bags in each hand and walked through the snow in -20 temperatures, one would think I was from an African Massabi or Indian village.

I was a coconut, who never wore a sari, never spoke Tamil, and did not understand Sri Lankan politics. I only ever went to Sri Lanka once for a week before getting married. I ate curry and rice with my hand too, but there was an assortment of other goodies in Sri Lankan cuisine. I acquired and developed my taste for Sri Lankan food. The parties where you were required to bring a dessert and have it judged seemed harmless enough. I recollected my own dessert; the first I made was a biscuit marshmallow concoction, and I left it on the huge dining table as a presentation. It was an eyesore. If anything, it was the worst dish. The corners of my mother-in-law's mouth turned up into a smile, and she did refrain from laughing. This was a Delia Smith family; they were food connoisseurs. There my dish stayed, and I watched to see whether anyone dared to take a bite.

At some point, the comparison moved from desserts to other talents and then to people in general, which made no one happy. Three of the daughters-in-law sewed their children's clothes, and some ventured as far as making wall-hanging art pieces using tapestry. Johanna, the eldest, was fast becoming her mother; as the next matriarch in line, she was grooming for her well-rehearsed role. She was always espoused to be *top dog* when it came to sewing, entertaining, intelligence, and cooking. She was the yardstick by which we were all compared, but luckily for me, I was not really in the race, as I lagged *way* behind. Which of the daughters-in-law were favoured and which had fallen from grace was a revolving door. But I guess a mother's love will always gravitate towards her own child, following the protective instincts of a fierce tiger mum.

Years later, I would think about the wastage of food – the leftovers that were divided among the family and then the rest packed in fridges and freezers. They were proud Tamils and not diluted culturally. I ate by hand too. It was the arrogance one has at the purity of a culture or the purity of a race or even the purity of a religion that excludes the other that I found distasteful.

I functioned at work, made meals for my family, washed the dishes, and paid bills. I went shopping and looked after my son and his numerous hospital, doctor, and psychotherapist visits. I would take out garbage, paint the rooms, and throw out furniture. My chores seemed endless, and there were times when I would have to walk quite a distance to do the shopping and still be expected to do other things when I returned home.

Once when Kumar was a baby, I came in from raking leaves and watering the grass to discover that he was crying; my tasks had prevented me from hearing, and I didn't know how long he'd been crying. I felt awful disappointment that all these things were happening. As our house was on a slope, all the neighbours' leaves were swept by the wind to my house. Whenever this happened, I would have to do a heap of raking – back-breaking work – that would result in over twelve bags of yard waste.

❧ ❧ ❧

Kumar's seventh birthday party took a lot of planning and preparation. Unfortunately, I had to walk to the shops to buy what I needed for the loot bags, as the buses were not running; it was a forty-five-minute walk each way. Even after everything was organised, I still had a lot of running around indoors to do before Kumar's friends arrived for the party. Finally, everything was set to go. Rays Reptiles was going to bring a host of amphibians, reptiles, and small creatures to the party. Kumar would show how fearless he was in front of his friends when the python was wrapped around him. I hurriedly set the cake aside, checked in to make sure the face painter would arrive on time, and finished filling the loot bags.

After the party, everyone went home. As I went to lie down on the couch, Andrew started saying that the weeds needed pulling, and I got up. I thought I was losing my mind. He was wearing, wearing, wearing me down, and I knew not why. I would go shopping early in the morning before anyone was up in order to avoid any tongue-lashing. I was working like a workhorse at home and had to be ready to be on show at family gatherings. Suddenly, I understood why the feminists had written their books. I understood the movie *To Kill a Mockingbird,* especially the ending, when Boo hides in the shadows after killing the man who wanted to kill the lawyer's children in an act of revenge. Taking Boo out of his surroundings and bringing him to justice would be like killing a mocking bird. Like Boo, I was a prop, a sideline character who was being pushed into centre stage. Years wasted on a bad marriage were the slow death of the mockingbird. What an epiphany! I totally got it. What other lies lurked beneath the facade?

The Family:
Outlaws

*A*ndrew's family was comprised of middle-class professional educated members of Mensa and people with money. He had four sisters and five brothers. It was no wonder the four girls were apt at doing household chores and versatile with a sewing needle and could cook for thirty people effortlessly. An abundance of food – different types of meats and at least three or four deserts – was always on the table. Did it seem obscene?

In the beginning, when I was a new bride, I had looked on the gourmet dinners served with enjoyment. Within five minutes, the new in-laws' community was trying to find out where I came from and if the guests were ever related to my family. This study of genealogy went so far as tracing marriages and Ammah's and Papa's places of birth. I never really understood why there was so much interest about my lineage until I myself wanted to know who my son's grandmother was.

This family loved to have parties in style, and to those who attended, it must have seemed like the family had a never-ending pit of money (it did to me) – my in-laws always supplied generous amounts of booze and food. No expense was spared for birthdays, wedding anniversaries, Thanksgiving, Christmas and Easter, and my hosts were hospitable hosts.

As Christmas approached, various family members would ask the usual questions: "Who's hosting Christmas this year?" "What about the Secret Santa?" And inevitably someone would say, "I am always the one doing this." After each return trip to Quebec, everyone living in

Quebec would head to the Sri Lankan store Babu's in Toronto to stock up on string hoppers, fish buns, Chinese rolls, and kothu roti. Andrew and I also stocked the fridges to save time and money. Andrew and I now had out Monday through Friday lunch menu for the week ahead.

My mother-in-law's self-esteem was strong, and her confidence, fuelled by years of her own brainwashing – "you're the best" – was unbreakable. That was a mantra my mother-in-law had primed her children with. They bought the press and believed that they were geniuses and beautiful.

My sisters-in-law were all five feet tall, with javelin-muscled broad shoulders and stocky builds. They were not the regular stereotypical magazine image of beauty, yet they walked tall, confident, and defiant. The eldest sister-in-law, Johanna, was the ruler, the yardstick upon which everyone else was measured; she was a Sophia Loren, a martini glass-type, the cocktail. She was the next matriarch in line. With these repeated aspirations – *I am the best* – everyone in Andrew's family grew to be confident, progressive human beings. Automatically, if you are the best, then someone has to be the worst. However, there were shortfalls in such brainwashing; an individual could lose his or her sense of self, his or her own thoughts, his or her own essence and individuality.

I was brought so far from my roots and so quickly – into a world of decadence, where women were intended to be the "hostess with the most", where one appetizer was not enough. More, more, more was the motto in this household. It was a world of social climbing and social networks that overlooked and marginalised the lonely. Every party with the community was an occasion for the red carpet, Oscar Night; the extravagance, the colours, and the scenes were taken straight from a blockbuster Bollywood Hindi movie.

Here, Andrew loved the centre stage. He had quite the twinkle toes for dancing and commanded the dance floor, whistling to Bangra music and swaying his hips like a Lambada dance. He could command the dance without a shadow of a doubt and received the applause for someone of his age to still be going the distance. He was the party animal.

It was at one of these show-off parties that I heard Michael Bublé's song "I Wanna Go Home", and it spoke deeply to me. It was as if Bublé had literally written her feelings; I listened to the lyrics: "And I feel just like I'm living someone else's life. / It's like I just stepped outside / when everything was going right.

Each month, each season, and each year was a repeat of sitting on the fence, not knowing how to change the shape of my relationship – a call for intimacy, a call for love and acceptance, a desire to finally feel *good enough* for Andrew and his family.

🦋 🦋 🦋

The in-laws were obsessed with Hindi movies – the sets, the saris, and the jewellery – where art imitated life, where someone was dying, someone loved someone who belonged to another, and someone lived with guilt or regret over something... The scenarios were endless. Whenever Aishwarya and the video clip of Chama Chama with the doe-eyed women swaying their hips on screen appeared on the television screen, my brothers-in-law would jump up and down in excitement. I never really heard of the Indian Bollywood Actor Shah Rukh Khan or the actress Rani Mukerjee but everyone in my in-laws seemed to know who they were. My in-laws had, strangely, alienated everyone from having a free life. They were all caught in living in their own bubble, an insular Victorian life.

I also enjoyed the movies; I understood the flavour of the shows through music and facial expressions, and thank heavens for subtitles.

🦋 🦋 🦋

The trips to and from Quebec to Toronto were quite the endless hurried routine. It was exhausting. Andrew would leave the radio on loud for the duration of the trip, so as to avoid conversations or arguments of a delicate nature. He drove at record speed, no doubt to arrive at his destination without having had to listen to me. I always sat in the back.

A birthday one weekend, a wedding the next, and if by chance there was a third obligatory visit that month, grumbling over gas prices and complaints of how tiresome it was to make the journey over and over again ensued.

🦋 🦋 🦋

When one of the sisters-in-law sewed an entire cover for the settee, I was left in awe of the workmanship. With enlarged eyes I piped to Dolly, "She sewed that by hand!"

I tried to sew a blouse and took sewing classes. The end product was that one sleeve was longer than the other. I accidentally cut a hole in the pants. In the end, I abandoned the idea. It was taking a whole lot of time, and it was not something I really wanted to learn.

Comfortable chic was just not good enough; here, getting lipstick on your teeth or forgetting to paint your toenails while wearing open toe shoes was a state of emergency. Dressing the whole nine yards was a must, obligatory for the entire extended family. They walked the part, like pseudo royalty. I remembered falling out of a van when attending a wedding in Sri Lanka. Andrew's uncle had remarked, "Even my eighty-three-year-old sister could step out of the van more elegantly." Never a truer statement was ever made. I knew my mother-in-law was elegant and walked the walk. My own son Kumar remarked, "Look at my appammah. Isn't she pretty?" I tried to dance their performance, but it was not natural to me. Not even a strand of hair dared be out of place, an order prevailing.

My in-laws were fiercely competitive and jealous like children. They bought bigger and bigger houses as "phallic symbols" to their strength. They appeared to have a strong sense for what was "right". They sent money for their poor cousins and went searching for their cousin who went missing. Yet in their own life, when "honour" came into the equation, they were misguided. "Honour" is perfection, and since none can honestly say we are perfect, what a useless commodity honour becomes for both the living and the dead. The size of the house does not make a home. What one chooses as his or her abode is irrelevant as long as it is furnished with peace and happiness and it is a safe place. Home can be a mansion, an apartment, a bedsit so long as you can be safe to heal.

My in-laws knew how to have joy at other's expense, teasing each other incessantly and laughing supportively at every punchline. I found it hard to accept the sarcasm or be awed at the quick wit, especially if it unwittingly hurt another. I had not grown up in a family that laughed, as my family's challenges had been altogether different from those my in-laws faced. We'd curbed any sarcasm in order to avoid provoking the other into a severe retaliation that inevitably involved the entire family. My home life was altogether a different one.

When my uncle wanted to visit from Malaysia, Andrew blocked this visit, saying that I was too ill to have visitors and that my uncle would see me ill. I was crumbling and overwhelmed by the pressure of doing everything, staying healthy, keeping up the facade for the community, and pleasing Andrew. I never questioned Andrew's decision to exclude my Uncle. My family never pushed for answers. I assumed the vanity of the family was more important than ensuring support for his wife. Human beings can be strategic about maintaining a status quo without considering how damaging what they are doing is for the other person. The family here, like so many characters in the movies, blocked and isolated not only me but Andrew too. They maintained their strength and control and dared no one to leave the fold of the family. This became a mechanism for keeping all the secrets intact and, more importantly, suppressing the will of the individual. It also explained why they kept up with traditional seasonal family camping trips. In some ways, the in-laws appeared to be progressive and forward looking, yet they were not broad-minded.

Now upon reflection, I realised that Andrew's decision not to allow my Uncle to visit was a calculated move to block all support from my family so that nothing would be revealed. There were, again, many compounding reasons for these blocks. I suspect Andrew was preventing my family from learning about the difficulties of my current situation. But he did attempt to call Hamza and indicate that things were not so smooth for me.

He could not openly be supportive as his allegiance was intricately woven with secrets, lies, and loyalty to his family. Perhaps on the flip side, Andrew was also preventing my family from learning about his family's secrets. There was never any doubt in my mind that, he was always preventing my family's past from tarnishing and contaminating his family. Every move was calculated and strategic. The in-laws, together with Andrew, needed to block all contact with my family so that my transformation would not be contaminated by my own dysfunctional family, as well as to obstruct my family from gaining any knowledge of their secrets and lies. Watching a killer whale play with its prey and toss the seal before devouring it, I saw the correlation between nature and human beings. When the lion pride isolates its prey, it chooses the weakest and takes it away from the herd. How reminiscent of my life. Now I saw, a further disturbing characteristic in nature, sharks in the water, were decapitating seals not necessarily for food. *Maybe*, this enjoyment for pain was always there, this thrill for destruction, power and control.

None of my immediate family ever wanted to visit me. There were eventually a few visits from England, but it took twelve years before Abijan came to visit. Did my family understand the unspoken message that they were not really wanted or welcomed? Or did they feel inadequate among the high achievers in Andrew's family?

I could understand why my sister-in-law, Stephen's wife, became the long-suffering martyr. She was avoidant and became silent. I understood her "I am equal to them or better than them" attitude. She knew their dark secrets. She refused to cook for her parents-in-law and stubbornly refused interactions with them at any level. It was a defensive mechanism and a powerful tool. What I found rather strange was that these in-laws practiced "forgiveness" almost as a poetic licence to say and do the nastiest things to each other. How long is a piece of thread and how many times must you forgive? *Give us all a break*, I thought.

Andrew would say. "You have a duty as a friend to tell another human being the truth if they have a booger hanging from their nose." What utter hogwash! What about the elephant in the living room? This was merely an excuse to belittle someone, emotionally destabilise him or her because you had some hold on him or her. You knew their Achilles heel. There was no repentance, and they were repeat offenders of mental and emotional abuse. My mother-in-law taught her children forgiveness as a wild card, but it should not be used as a wild card to excuse continual wrongdoings.

While greed and selfishness may have been strongly characteristic in my family, selfishness, vanity, and ego were inherently vibrant in Andrew's family. If I did an economist's numbers game, I would ruminate that if one person had to sacrifice his life for nine other members of the family, why was it hard for the nine to sacrifice something of their vanity to let the one have his own life, his own happiness? Happiness is surely a measure of success. I understood that I needed my freedom to be happy. Ammah, now on the other side, understood this too.

I was zombified, scared, lost in big houses, social events with Sri Lankans, associating with the "haves it all" and "have-nots". Andrew wanted me to buy into the idea that no conspiracy theory existed and that his family really loved me. If they loved me, how come I did not feel it? Their Tamil voices were loud and filled the rooms with self-importance, a projection of unwavering confidence, an echo that returned. Why when I attended all these gatherings with my in-laws didn't anyone want to talk to me? I was depressed, but yes, you could have a relationship with a mentally ill person. I attempted to talk to the hostess and others, but they ignored me, so I busied myself with my child. But I was always attentive of the stage, my role, and the people invited into this world. I felt like an oddity, a piece of furniture being moved from room to room. I was a misfit.

I self-censored; I governed myself by a hidden rule that silence was the most excellent way to survive in this family. If you revealed too much, things would be used against you, would become the proverbial Achilles heel. I witnessed open criticism of my sister-in-law Dolly, who was depressed and unhappy. These comments usually came from the eldest sister-in-law, Johanna, or my mother-in-law, who would openly criticise her, saying things like, "You fed your child burgers, fast food." "You don't wipe your child's face when he has a snotty nose." "You leave your child in dirty diapers far too long." These comments merely translated to "You are not a good enough mother." Or at least that was the way I understood them.

Who is the Head of the Family?

Andrew would taunt me and attack my brother, saying he had no work ethic and was "stupid". He would predict where it would all end up – the demise of Balram. I was all too aware of the truth surrounding my family's imperfections, but I was caught in the birth order, and being a middle child and a woman, I did not challenge or rock the boat.

I once gave Ammah a simple test, asking, "Ammah, whose telephone number do you remember?" With every child, Ammah drew a blank. But when I said Balram's name, Ammah remembered his telephone number by rote and never even hesitated. He was, without a doubt, her number one pet, and Balram grieved and grieved for his loss when Ammah died. Ammah was spent with her suffering, drained by the business called life. The fight of her youthful days was so far in the past. All that Ammah had gone through stayed with me. It was an odds game for any mother: How would her children turn out? Ammah's faith in God and Balram was steadfast. She only ever wanted Balram to be the head of the family.

I felt weighed down by the family's lack of independence and lack of self-sufficiency. I wished my family members were self-reliant and could manage to curb their greed and selfishness. It was not such a dreadful thing to sacrifice a want for the need of another. It made complete sense. Sometimes, I felt the need for justice, fairness and other times, just a phone call. I would send money home and hoped that some benefit would trickle down to my mother. Secretly, Ammah wanted it to be Balram to be the giver. In the end, it didn't matter who was the giver as long as the need was met. I had to accept that there were times I was unable to be there, to be the giver and the helper.

Andrew and Balram were constantly at loggerheads with each other. In reality, they avoided each other because they were really mirror images of what the other desired and that was reflected back to them. It was a competition – the newcomer versus the firstborn. Andrew was always seeking the centre stage and approval. This was primarily why my husband could not get along with my brother; they both sought the esteemed title of "head of the family" after Papa died. Both loved the centre stage and to have their voices heard.

Andrew could not relax because he was living a lie and was undercover. He took pride in working every day, and he never allowed himself a sick day. He was rigid and regimental because he did not know how to relax; he had been primed for this stage all his life. Balram resented his brother-in-law because he was an engineer with a regular pay cheque and, to his mind, a "fool", a slave to society, a clog in the wheel, a pleaser rather than a controller. Balram was going to make millions and aim for beyond the coconuts. To Balram, the control over the family was his by birthright, but at Ammah's death, this would be a burdensome title. Everyone from Malaysia and Singapore rang him to offer condolences. He was the "go-to man", and he had to pass their wishes to the rest of the family. He had a hard time grieving in peace.

I sat in this uncomfortable hot seat. They both could not set aside their spirit of competition to get along.

I Love You, I Love You Not

The family was good and, at times, supportive. When Kumar was born, I stayed with Jessie and Alfred, and they took care of me and the baby; Jessie showed me how to hold the baby and bathe him and tended to my scar. I knew she was also caught in the hot seat – the shifting revolving door that could eventually lead her "down to the gallows".

My fortieth birthday was approaching, and I silently hoped that my in-laws would throw a party for me. I thought that turning forty was a milestone. It was not as if my in-laws did not know what I had left behind, and, secretly, they all knew what I had as a "marriage". Andrew's brothers were jealous of their parents' fondness for me and not their wives. Wishing secretly for a celebration was silly really, because birthdays are for children. The day passed without anyone noticing, unacknowledged.

Mistakenly, I told Andrew that I'd thought his family would have had a party. Later, the family made a display on another day, and there were balloons, lots of balloons – another demonstration to mock me, to show me that parties were really for small children. This was the message, and it was loud and clear. I felt small and foolish. It hurt, but cruel intentions were second nature to the clan, and I knew they knew no other way. A parallel life in the movie Cruel Intentions, I was being punished for something that I had no part in. In fact, I suspect he could not punish his abuser.

My mother-in-law said, "Why are you doing this to her?"

No one seemed to answer.

Andrew attempted to get even or at least strike back for this "put-down". He would, at the next few birthdays, have his son blow out all the candles, no matter whose birthday it was, the old and young alike. Kumar would have been quite old with the number of candles he blew out that year.

I could not understand how a simple desire to celebrate my fortieth birthday could create such public display of the ridiculous. It took time, but I forgave this and moved with the mantra, "go with the flow".

Everyone kept espousing that I was loved, but apparently that "love" wasn't great enough to cause anyone to tell me the truth about why my marriage was what it was. They did not love me enough to tell me why my husband was angry so that I could stop running myself to the ground trying to please him. I got hurt too; I had years robbed from me. I wanted to scream to Ammah, *They tethered me to an angry man and did not tell me why he was so angry.* Twelve years is a long time.

🦋 🦋 🦋

Another party rolled around, and this time it was for Andrew's eldest brother, Patrick, the family preacher whose diabetes was attacking his system due to a culmination of stress and an unhealthy diet. He, like Balram, dreamed of a millionaire's life. Patrick's fiftieth birthday arrived, and his wife Mariana, who loved food and shopping, was "voluntold" by the family to organise a party for him. The family wanted to celebrate all their siblings' milestones.

Mariana was a skinny woman and quite amazing really, for she had given birth to four girls, and it was quite a job raising them. She was a fellow Malaysian, and she never rose past the fact that she kept her family's rendang recipe away from Johanna. Jessie was teasing Mariana and asked why she did not receive an invitation to the party by a phone call. Mariana just rolled her eyes and remarked, "She wants a special invitation." I suppose, Mariana just thought that, when you are family, you did not need an invite; it was just assumed you would be included.

I wore the dress Andrew's sister Johanna had picked for me when we went shopping. It was a Marilyn Monroe, red polka dot dress with a halter neck. It was not really glamorous, but when I wore it, it showed my ample bosom and my bare back. If Johanna had chosen this dress and Andrew approved, I could be confident that the family would approve. Johanna would not set me up to fall. The understudy was surely well prepared.

In fact, when I arrived at the party, my sister-in-law, Shalini, remarked, "You are a hot mama." I smiled. The dress was not really was my style; rather, I was fulfilling Andrew's expectation of me. I was, at the very least, costumed for my part. Then the cameraman, Mark, the youngest brother, came and started taking photos of me in an attempt to mock me. He glanced and rolled his eyes at Johanna, and she smirked. No snide remarks were necessary; it was a visual display announcing that I was not this great beauty. I did not consider myself as outshining the other women at the party.

I was hurt again, hurt that my brother-in-law could do this. He was the last person I would think would partake in such a display; he was the one with the skinny latte complexion who'd attended my engagement in England – the neutral guy, who did not look for trouble.

🦋 🦋 🦋

On another occasion, at the time of Indran's death – he was the first member of the family to cross over – the family respected the customary one-year grieving period and abstained from having a Christmas party for their father. They howled and wailed. When you cry, you really cry for yourself – for how badly you feel.

I knew my mother-in-law was basically a good person, but after years of standing by her man, she'd grown harder and harder, desensitised to the abuse until it became the new normal. When her husband died, she cried so hard – they all wailed – and I wondered if his death was a release for all the pain and suffering my mother-in-law too had endured in her own marriage.

My mother-in-law was now free to dress as she wanted. On now she had wasted time – the greatest commodity.

I came a day later to be with the family. At Stephen's house, a rectangular billboard displayed a collage of family photos, recalling a life lived and past moments. Because I'd been tardy, the family retaliated, including only one small picture of me and my husband and none of Kumar, the grandson. It was hard not to see this omission as deliberate, especially when all the other grandchildren were there. It was a case of someone in the family choosing who he or she liked and including the photos accordingly. It was another public snub. The family recovered with the excuse that they could not find any photos of Kumar.

I said to Andrew, "My child is not family."

It took time, but I forgave and again recalled the mantra – "go with the flow".

I helped as best I could and made sure my sister-in-law had food to eat. I tried to do what I could. My personal best might well not have been the Devadas' best, but I did it with warmth and compassion. I knew death personally. I overheard my youngest sister-in-law, Celine, say, "Ah poor thing, doing all that." And then Alfred said, "Never mind, when her mother dies, we can do the same." He paused and then added, "And when her son dies."

I was angry. How dare someone, never mind an uncle, say this? It seemed such an odd and misplaced comment to make.

I tried to love them all like my own brothers and sisters. Secretly, I knew that they really did not love me as they professed. It was the reason I listened to conversations, to know how to navigate in the family.

🦋 🦋 🦋

It was playtime again, the cat-and-mouse game. This time, I was at Alfred and Jessie's house. After eating Jessie's meal, Stephen, the younger brother, the butterball comedian in the family, wanted to strike a low blow. Like the cat with the cream cheese and butter, he smiled and insisted that I stay and watch a movie.

"What is it about?" I asked.

"A conspiracy movie," was the only reply.

I was sleepy and tired. I wanted to go home but did not want to disappoint him. Again following my mantra of going with the flow, I stayed. The movie was *Shutter Island*, and Leonardo DiCaprio played a war veteran who arrives at a fortress-like island housing a hospital for the criminally insane. Everyone watched me as the movie played and smiled smugly at one another. Some were more interested in watching my reaction than the movie, smiling in a way that appreciated Stephen's daring. I looked back at them and thought they had to be kidding. Did they believe it was remotely possible that I could be expected to sit through the entire movie? When someone was suffering, why would anyone do this?

I kept looking back at my brothers-in-law and sisters-in-law, wondering if they really knew the pain they had caused. Was it deliberate? Of course it was; it was a movie night for the Devadas; they got to watch someone become emotionally disturbed and destabilised, and they took pleasure in it. I now realized that they were really not interested in comedy, the play of words and action was to belittle, humiliate and degrade socially, emotionally and mentally.

I wanted to think that this was not deliberate. If someone knew how much baggage you carried from the past, your cross, would they sit on the cross as you struggled to carry it? I wanted to give them the benefit of the doubt, the possibility that no malicious intent was meant. I questioned the choice of movie as a first-year law student would, I knew the content was enough to prove intent. And the act was compounded when no one stopped the film from playing.

Halfway through the movie, Andrew looked at me and suggested it was time to leave. I did not want to be destabilised. I stayed for a while longer, but when it became clear that the movie was about patients in a hospital dealing with post-traumatic stress disorder and other mental anxieties, I knew my in-laws had crossed over to a new level of cruelty.

I gave my ring to Andrew, and when he asked me why, I replied, "If you need to ask, then really there is no marriage."

Later, I took my wedding ring back and began again to work at my marriage. Karma dealt the card, and soon Stephen was depressed and suddenly neither he nor his family saw the funny side of mental illness.

❦ ❦ ❦

The family home movies were just one of the ways they could score points or play games. Another way was making incisive dumbass comments in passing. They were not courageous enough to be up front and open. I was called "Anti I", to show that I had no fun, a play on words as I was known as Aunty. At college, I'd found other Sri Lankan friends and had found that they could make a poor Norwegian man blush, though at times, I would be caught off-guard in embarrassing situations and fall into the stereotype of a blushing Indian. Isn't it funny that is it not the similarities that resemble one another but the differences. I think it was Levis Strauss who said this.

For this type of humour, a huge audience was required, as the Achilles heel was the punchline in the family. Did I lack a sense of humour? I doubted myself again. Of course, you can have laughter when the environment is safe and there is trust. I could laugh, but honestly I had not grown up in a family where you could bring the house down with laughter.

Whatever I did, my husband's family were there to judge my intentions, to judge my motivations for my actions. If I gave a birthday card and professed to steer my niece to love, it was met with jeers and open disapproval. If I helped wash the dishes, someone would comment, "There she goes, trying to show she is good."

I was not good. I had smoked a joint of "wacky-backy" and drank alcohol like it was mother's milk. Sometimes, having a stiff drink was the Dutch courage I needed to stay relaxed and enjoy those parties. I was damned if I did and damned if I didn't – this, no doubt, happened to us all. God, no doubt, was busier with more important things than how much I drank, the wacky-backy, or my sins of the past. I never looked at these as sins, only in excess; I risked losing my free will and giving another person. I pondered over my own position, a dichotomy of nature, where I was two sides of a coin.

I am good, and I am bad
I am forgiving, and I am unforgiving

77

I am crazy, and I am sane
I am healed, and I am unhealed

The surrounding substance of the divine is that I am a sinner who chooses my own path, the journey. It matters not the path chosen, only that I am happy, for what makes me happy is a self-awareness of my purpose. I only need navigate my life not hurting another. In the timeline of life, there is always redemption, so long as it is heartfelt and sincere. God's ear hears all, and he sees the heart of a prostitute, a stripper, an abused homosexual, and an insignificant nobody. If he hears your prayers, why would he not hear their prayers?

The Son We Had!

*D*ear darling boy, Kumar, the day the contractions started, your appah showed us a rainbow in the sky as we drove to the hospital. He bought you a greyish blue pram, brand spanking new. You were born just missing Canada Day, by C-section. Even in the beginning, your appah was hands on with a crying baby, pacing up and down the ward, trying to hush you to sleep. God had other plans, and you arrived the next day, missing the fireworks you could have had every year on your birthday.

Ammah could not hold you, as I was recovering from the epidural. All I could do was sing lullabies to let you know that I was there, present, and accounted for. There was this space between us, from the bed to the cot. Ammah could not move to carry you, paralyzed by the epidural and waiting anxiously for its effects to wane.

When you heard Ammah's voice, your head moved, looking for the sound. You were born with big flat feet like your appah's. When your body temperature dropped, the nurses rushed in and placed you on my chest. When you were allowed out, you barely fitted in your car seat, being only five pounds eight ounces.

Your appah loved you so and would take the hairdryer and blow-dry you just to keep you warm. At social parties, he held you in his arms, dressed in his dinner suit and armed with a milk bottle in his jacket pocket. He spoilt you rotten, and not a slap did you ever receive. Ammah would play John Lennon's "Beautiful Boy" and hold you. You were far from cute, and your cries were *ilai ilai*.

I did everything I was supposed to do for Kumar and took him to all his doctor's visits. It was at the children's doctor's office that I read the words, "Children learn what they live", a quote by Dorothy Law Nolte, posted on the wall, and it spoke to me strongly. Initially, while Kumar was a baby, I did not pay attention to these words, as I was trying to make Kumar eat his food. Being of small build, Kumar had everyone guessing whether he was malnourished. I would use a turkey baster to pump food into him. His doctor kept minimising my concerns, saying, "You are not tall; he is following his own growth curve."

In the patient room, I focused on some of the lines:

> If a child lives with criticisms,
> He learns to condemn.
>
> If a child lives with hostility,
> He learns to fight.

I wanted to create a new environment, a world vastly different from the one I'd walked into, from the one I'd left. I knew that, quite possibly, my son might be depressed and would struggle with learning. I was all too aware of my mother's life, my own journey, and not being able to help my own past background.

I tried to help Kumar early on. I did not want my mother's life. My son was my reason for living, my purpose, and why I stayed. Together, we found places of interest; we went to Disney on Ice, skating, Winterlude. We would go to see the dinosaurs in the Museum of Nature and to participate in many other fun activities.

I was bitter about my mother/son relationship because most of the time, I was distracted by a rage, I lost the best years of my son's life on a focus of a bad relationship and he would bear the brunt of witnessing the two of us at each other.

I did not want to instil in Kumar the mandate, "honour thy father and thy mother", because over the years, this could become self-worship and adoration of my son, who I would "own". I wanted Kumar to fulfil his dreams and his wishes. I merely wanted to be a guardian of the spirit for his destiny, and his will to choose should never be clouded; otherwise his life would be as empty as the cow's dried milk.

Andrew:
No Way Out!

Reflecting back into the past, I noted that Andrew was depressed. He was unhappy and anxious, and I did not know what was bothering him. When we went to Shoppers Drugmart, I held back and browsed the aisles for things I could buy. Andrew went to the pharmacist desk and filled a prescription for antidepressants. I was distressed and disappointed. I thought I had escaped my own family's bag of issues. How was I going to make him happy and stop the anger?

Andrew would stay downstairs and sleep on the couch. He seemed to like his own company and, again, I never questioned why Andrew felt the need to escape in sleeping. These bouts of withdrawal from my son and I were alienating. I made the excuse that it was not personal. He was a Tamil man allowing himself the odd break away from the family. Under my own delusion, I rationalised everything – I was not a true-blue Sri Lankan.

Andrew was not intimate with me. When I cuddled him, he would turn his back. My son would sleep in between us, almost as an accepted physical barrier for intimacy. I would turn to him to fill my void of love and acceptance.

Every weekend, I felt the urge to leave the house. I probably picked up on the clue that I was not needed at home and that Andrew needed to sleep on the couch. I made friends quickly and took my son with me at all times so that the crying child would not bother Andrew. I signed up for music for tots and visited my friends who had children and would only return home late afternoon. I kept myself busy with activities for my son, and even when my friends asked Andrew to come along for the ride, he always had the pretext of work.

Andrew watched TV, and I took my son to bed so that he was free to relax. I felt his disinterest and his neglect. I did not pick up on the clue that he did not want to be with me, did not want to have a relationship with me. I felt alone in my marriage, and my mother-in-law; my brother-in-law Stephen; and Johanna, the eldest sister-in-law, stepped up to fill a void. I now realised their unique role in my life. They were supporters and the distraction for me, and I could not focus on my own relationship, only the entourage. Andrew needed the entourage; he was incapable of having a relationship or able to sustain a relationship with me.

Even a simple phone call would bring about anger, frustration, and short cutting remarks to put me down. Obviously, he didn't even want to talk to me. I had to keep my distance. He would shout me down and silence my voice with his outbursts. Soon the conversations on the phone were merely to run the household chores; marriage had become a family business.

I attempted to do everything before Andrew came home so as to avoid the verbal assault. He was the "barking dog" that you would be afraid to pet. The outbreak and flare-up of a repressed rage were directed at me, and the greatest excuse was my depression. It was merely projection; he really could not come out with the real reason for his anger, frustration, and disappointment. Truly, there was never a good time for a conversation.

Clueless again, I tried to navigate around Andrew's unprovoked anger and his disinterest in me. I filled my void with outings with my friends and their children, and whenever I asked him to join us, he merely hid under the excuse of working late.

When Andrew was not espousing my talents for the entourage of bystanders, he would take some pleasure in humiliating me. Whenever the family entourage was present, Andrew would go into an almost well-rehearsed spin, boasting and promoting my accomplishments and my qualities. I could not understand why he felt the need to put me out there.

The family was continually espousing how fortunate I was to get Andrew. There were, after all, a number of female suitors who all wanted Andrew. I was the lucky chosen one! Andrew wanted a tall woman, a cook, an educated woman, a working wife, a cleaner, and a mother to his child.

I remembered Papa's conversation with Balram about when he'd chose Ammah. Papa said, "I looked to see if she was going to be a good mother to my children and would look after me in my old age."

Andrew had convinced himself that I was the one for him; he lied to himself and had to have the entourage support him because, deep down inside, he knew he had made a mistake. I did not have a relationship with Andrew, so it was understandable that I felt insecure with other women.

Early on in our relationship, I was introduced to a few of Andrew's lady friends from his past, who were either interested in him or who wanted to marry him. Frankly, I thought I had every right to be confident. I had married him.

At one Sri Lankan party, I met a glamorous woman who was my sister-in-law's best friend and who was apparently keen on marrying Andrew in the past. The family brought her into the inner sanctum. I wished I could laugh it off. It was as if they were deliberately attempting to shove me out of the family circle. Andrew seemed to push me farther and farther to the back of the hall, and he hesitated in introducing her to me. I wanted to know why he felt the need to avoid any confrontation or explanation. Was he embarrassed about this or did he have something to hide? It seemed like a harmless tease, and if I were confident about my relationship, I would have been able to brush this aside. I was insecure.

I made excuses, telling myself that the family wasn't deliberately attempting to sabotage or destabilise an already rocky marriage. To the outside world, it looked solid. In front of me stood a tall, beautiful, and successful woman who earned $100,000 a year. In fairness, I assumed the world did not know that I had a rocky relationship.

I had bottled things up all my life. I could not understand the hidden agenda or hidden message. I suspected, though, that the display was a not-so-subtle message to Andrew that his wife was not really all he espoused her to be, that, in truth there were greater beauties and more worthy women. I knew this to be true. To compete for the love of your husband is a useless thing, for if you must compete, he was never yours in the first place.

I would face more similar episodes at other family gatherings. Andrew would disappear with a lady friend at a party while I sat at the table with his relatives. This did not go unnoticed by the crowd at the party. It was obvious to everyone at the table that he was flirting, and one of his relatives said, "Ah, Andrew…"

I would sit motionless, pretending that I did not notice what was happening, a feigned attitude of nonchalance my only defence. As the music played and Andrew returned from his sneaky tête-à-tête, one of his cousins kindly offered to dance with me to save face. This was a public slap of many to come.

On another occasion, at Stephen's house, Andrew talked incessantly with a girl whose conversation he found interesting. I felt his disinterest, and the gulf between us widened. With his arm demonstratively around this other woman, Andrew piped, "When your wife leaves you, you can always find another woman to hug."

How true! It was better to be alone for the right reasons than to be with someone for all the wrong ones. I felt hurt and woke up in the night and slapped him for insulting me in front of everyone. This he would use to relabel me as crazy.

Homosexuals are comfortable with women and even more so when they are under cover and protected with a ring on the third finger. Andrew and I were just on different wavelengths, not at all on the same frequency, and no amount of coaching or fine-tuning would ever set us down the same path. I reflected that this was possibly a result of his living a lie that was slowly eating him. I would witness his rage directed at his mother. It was such a misplaced display because "mothers" were revered; disrespecting one's mother was a cultural "no-no".

Andrew was always blaming me and scolding me for the lack of intimacy. He would say things like, "You are ill, and I looked after you!" and, "Who would want to come home to you?" "I cooked for you," he would say, or, "I could not retire with you."

Such statements were so truthfully spoken. He did cook for me. Cooking was his forte, as natural as his Tamil singing. But sometimes eating would be hard because of his mental and emotional abuse. Again there was a disconnect between caring for someone and abusing them.

When I asked him to come to my friend's party, he went but alluded to the fact that I was some kind of airy-fairy person, whose friends were equally the same and not really his type. He complained about being there. This was not an isolated occasion. The same thing happened every time I asked him to go with me to visit my friends. He would promptly take control over the conversation, using the opportunity to discuss how victimised he was, by having to live with his "sick wife". He was unhappy and blamed his me for the mess he had got himself in.

I witnessed many outbursts of temper in my twelve years with Andrew. Once he wanted to stomp his sister because she'd compared him to a cat and then proceeded to say she loved the cat more. He wanted to hit me with the bottle too but never did. He tried to strangle me because I wanted to have conversation with him at odd hours of the day. He had an unprovoked anger that was explosive, and every so often even when accidents happened, like the car getting stuck in the snow, a torrent of unkind words would fly from his mouth. "couldn't you see the snowbank and why would you drive over it" he yelled. It was his opportunity to vent because he had to come outside and shovel the snow. He had to help me get the car out of the snowbank.

I did not mean to get the car into the ditch or have the car break down outside Food Basic. I felt incompetent, incapable of having a smooth life, where keys were not lost, cars did not break down, and I did not leave my lunch at home. These were moments of ordinariness that could happen to "anyone", but I felt that I had brought this anger upon myself by not being organised and failing and failing. Andrew was caught in a physically aging body with diabetes and his own depression attacking his system.

Physically, Andrew had the body of a middle-aged man, but he was mentally years younger, trying to "make it" out there. He, like all of us, had that all-illusive dream children have of saying "look at me". He was Peter Pan. He could never grow up. I was aging too. Andrew would often excuse his anger by pointing to the fact that his mother had accidently poured hot water over him as a child. He hated water and had refused to have a bath after that incident. I could never understand how a child could remember this. There had to be more to blame for the type of anger I saw in Andrew. Andrew was constantly seeking approval; he wanted to be the best son, the best husband, and the trophy "go-to man". He played the "big man", solver of all problems.

Andrew's belief that he had sacrificed for his family came clearly into the light one day at Alfred's house when Andrew exploded at his nieces and nephews. "I have done a lot for you all," he told them. "I made a sacrifice, and you do not appreciate it." This was quite a revelation.

Jessie chased her girls upstairs, and I was again clueless about the reason for the outburst. I had made my own sacrifice, but I was not about to pin this on my nephew and niece in England. The nephews and nieces were shocked and upset, and I was stupefied.

Later, I would come to understand that marriage with me was burdensome for Andrew, and he resented the enforced role he had to play to assure that his nieces and nephews would marry in the elite circles. Another light bulb flashed.

Back in London, England

I made a number of visits to England to see my family during my twelve years of marriage. A spirit of the transient filled the air in London. This was a historical city, but I would see new developments. Westfield Shopping Centre sprouted up; the Oyster Card had been introduced; and now it cost fifty pence to use the public toilets, a far cry from the copper one penny the toilets had cost in the past. Chicken Tikka has long been the popular national dish in England. I love a good ole English Roast with Yorkshire pudding. In between all my visits, I discovered that the lady in the pharmacy had died. My friends had moved on and found other friends, and I felt the gap emotionally. No one wanted to waste a phone call on all the bad things going in their lives. Everyone I talked to merely said things like, "Oh, I'm fine." My friends all knew that we could do nothing to help each other when we were living miles apart. I used to miss my Walkers' cheese and onion and prawn cocktail crisps, the galleries, and the wine bars and coffee shops, but now I ate Lays and Poutine.

These changes merely served to remind me of my absence. It wasn't just the physical distance that separated my own siblings and me; the span of time away kept us unconnected.

Balram, Hamza, Abijan, and Ammah had their own individual journeys; none of them had the time or inkling to look at each other's pain. Their own pain consumed them. My own immigrant experience, my isolation as a wannabe high achiever, and my failure at pleasing

Andrew created an unwelcome resentment and discord that had rooted in my heart. I could not understand my sibling's indifference, but when someone is in pain, it's hard to see another's pain as greater. Greed and selfishness meant that the takers continued to take.

I was continually apologising for my sister, my brothers, and my mother. It wasn't blind faith or delusion. My automatic defence of them was rooted in my belief that no one should be allowed to stomp on someone else who was clearly in pain.

Ammah lacked the savvy for her survival, but her desire was to see all her children happy and doing whatever pleased them. I walked with my head down and eyes on the pavement, burdened by the stigma of mental illness and my family's imperfections.

Expert One:
The Cultural colluder

I walked into my family doctor's office in 2005, five years after my marriage, and spouted out, "My in-laws and I do not seem to get along, and the family is always talking about everyone. I am alone without my family, and Andrew is a hard man to please. He is always angry, and I do not know what really is kicking off his anger." I was overwhelmed by my life. I'd been fired from work and was struggling to fulfil my dream of becoming a lawyer. I felt so alone. I was worn down by the regime of keeping Andrew happy or navigating myself out of harm's way.

Dr Manjit asked about the family background, and when it was revealed that Fathima had taken her own life, the doctor's automatic response was, "I will recommend you to a psychiatrist; he is our own kind and will understand our culture."

It was only years later that I would come to understood this statement. Dr Manjit was offering a psychiatrist who would have no qualms about medicating me, so long as I stayed in my marriage, a culturally accepted norm. Understanding the culture meant just that – you stayed. My psychiatrist would give me a diagnosis that fitted my family genetic background but made no allowances for what I had to live with. My environment at home was stressful, and I was living on high adrenalin with an abusive person with an unleashed temper.

Dr Surjit, my psychiatrist, started me on a cocktail of medications, some of which only made my weight pile on. And I felt like I was on speed, doing the housework in half the time. It was trial and error with the drugs. My doctor was an Indian guy with the same poker face no matter what I told him. He listened to my story, and I recounted it, in the hope that he would tell me it was an isolated incident that had brought me to his office.

I said, "I think I am having a breakdown."

The doctor laughed and said, "No."

I'd thought it best to bring along my friend, Jasmine, who was a medical doctor from England, for moral support. Dr Surjit seemed slightly off guard, unsettled, until my friend revealed she was a medical doctor of infectious diseases and not another psychiatrist.

He proceeded to tell me, "You will have to be on these pills for life; mental illness or depression is like diabetes." He diagnosed me with schizo-affective disorder, but I knew that there was a study on epigenetics that had an opposing view. I was not kept hostage by my genetics but by the age old-debate of nature verses nurture.

The Many Noses
of Cyrano de Bererac

My mother-in-law coached her son, telling him how to date me. Walks to the park were her suggestion. Flowers, cards, and gifts were all mandatory – an acceptable norm for the front. He merely felt irritated that he had to be there. I would walk with him, but he seemed to want to be *somewhere else*. For him, these walks were an obligatory exercise that left me questioning the uselessness of his "efforts". At the park, he looked bored, restless, and uninterested and almost seemed to hate her. This was obligation for him – a task that he hated doing – being left alone with his wife. He just could not do relationships.

When Nasreen showed up to spend some time with me, she happily told me about her husband giving her a pair of lovely earrings. Nasreen beamed with pride over the gift, her face alight with a glow that came from knowing she had a man who loved and appreciated her, and her smile reached her eyes.

My mother-in-law piped to my husband, "See, you should learn from him." My mother-in-law wanted her son to be more forthcoming. But how do you love when your heart just isn't there?

Stephen would also coach his brother from the sidelines, prompting him to remember all his wife's good qualities, as if that would be enough to keep him from running from his obligation called "marriage". The brothers shared a hidden goal, to appease each other's spouses. My husband would make sure his sister-in-law, Dolly, was well fed when she was pregnant, and Stephen would take time to talk to me.

When I was pregnant with Kumar, I had to continue working extra hours in order to accumulate enough paid time to qualify for the government's one-year paid maternity leave. I was not eating well, and my husband was oblivious. His concern was making sure his pregnant sister-in-law Dolly, Stephen's wife, was fed. He wanted to appease Stephen and Dolly's marriage. In return Stephen, unbeknown to me, was appeasing my own failing marriage. I felt ignored. I would try to converse with Andrew, but he wanted no conversation or small talk. Ultimately, the only talk he seemed to engage in was the running of the house and managing my son. Stephen was the coach who continually reiterated all the reasons Andrew should stay.

It had been many years now, and I still sat in the back seat of the car with Kumar, who was fast growing out of his car seat. Stephen one day remarked, "Why don't you sit in the front." His eyes turned down, he was coaching a physical closeness that did not now exist. You can only have deep relationships with people who want them.

The Outlaw Madness — The Rape of the Mind

*A*fter twelve years of marriage, suddenly my mother-in-law wanted to reveal something to me, but she was scared. In truth and in fairness, she did not know how to approach the subject, having left it dormant for so long. She knew I had a son and had a right to the information. She kept repeating, "She has a son, and she has a right to know." From house to house she went, soliciting permission to reveal the secret. Then she would be forced back into silence by the rest of the family, confessing that she had nine other children to worry about and consider. It was only later on that I would discover that she did not want to reveal Celine as her husband's child but, rather, to tell me that her son was a homosexual and that, quite possibly, I would have to deal with this as a reality when Kumar matured. As a consequence, the comedy or nightmare began with one screwball after another.

Quite a few years back, I recalled a car trip from Toronto to Quebec when Andrew and his youngest sister, Celine, were talking. Celine was the soufflé, a tomboy who was groomed into a princess, and she drew her strength from the family. "Your mother is different from mine in that she does things…"

I had been dumbfounded. I was accidentally privy to information that was meant for the inner sanctum circles. I stayed silent and pretended to be asleep. It was not that I intentionally wanted to eavesdrop, but being one of four passengers in a car, the validity of eavesdropping was not really relevant here. I could not accept as true such a curve ball. I kept quiet. It really had nothing to do with me who Celine's mother was. I never mentioned to anyone what had been revealed.

I thought that, perhaps, there could be another child from my father-in-law's affairs. One evening, while clearing away the dishes, I told Andrew what I suspected and said what was on my mind. "I feel there are more Devadas out there."

"No," was his reply. "My mother only gave birth to nine."

What was Andrew trying to tell me? There were ten Devada children. Immediately, my thought turned to my son. I started crying, shocked and numbed. How was I going to tell my son that, quite possibly, the grandmother he knew might not actually be his grandmother and that his real grandmother might well be another person entirely? I didn't know how I was going to protect my son from people pointing and saying, "I know who your grandmother is, and it is not that woman." I was shocked to my core. It was an emotional punch. Everything I knew to be real was turned upside down.

It wasn't actually like me to cry on a whim. Yet, there I sat on the couch, immobilised by the curve ball of life, the slap in the face. To understand me is to understand my desire to have the truth. When walking in truth, you do not play games and you have real relationships. I was free spirited and did not want be caged by society or community because it was repressive. Repression was a dirty word for me because it hurt people mentally and emotionally. Conformity repressed the soul. I wanted Kumar to be brought up in the same way, to be true to himself, to live with what you cannot change and to be accepting of the unusual but to always walk in truth.

A few days later, at a local Chinese restaurant, the family gathered around to celebrate Alfred's birthday. He was the defender of the Tamil cause, and he hankered to be taken seriously as a leader in the family. His even-toned voice beguiled everyone, and all followed the even-toned voice of reason. It was odd to be present and accounted for at the restaurant and still not know who Kumar's grandmother was. Andrew tried to persuade me that I was too sensitive and that no one was "out to get me" – that the family loved me. "You can trust me," he told me. "I am your husband, and I will tell you when you are being sensitive. You are imagining things."

Alfred was pretty upset about the "big mouth Andrew" and let it be known at the table. Alfred's passing reference to his brother's slip of the tongue was constrained; he appeared to be logical, rational, and equally balanced, and I suspected that his even-toned voice was misleading. He was a fool leading a mass with another false consciousness, his even-toned voice. I recollected the trip to Toronto when Celine had first brought out the secret and piped my own contribution. "There were a number of big mouths before the one big mouth," I said in defence of Andrew.

When my mother-in-law confronted me about where I'd gotten such a story, I told the truth and said from Andrew.

Later at the house of Stephen, the fourth son and the prankster, I was again questioned about this. I told the truth.

This brought about reactive anger, and Andrew burst out, "You are crazy. You have schizo-affective disorder, and you imagined all this."

I was sure that he had alluded to the fact his mother had given birth to nine children, rather than the ten. I defended my mental health, my position, reasserting what I'd stated earlier, "You said this; you told me." I added, "I also heard Celine and your conversation." There was nothing wrong with having overheard.

I was starting to be scared though, afraid that, quite possibly, my illness was progressively worse. Was I becoming my brother? Had what I seen and heard really happened? Would I remember this as a vision or something I'd imagined or something that hadn't actually happened the next day? Andrew badgered me with this label, one I'd received from the first psychiatrist I'd seen. It was a convenient alibi. I was not crazy. I just didn't trust certain people, and like Charles Boyer in *Gaslight*, I had to keep my eyes wide open and my ears piqued to hear all conversations.

I began to suspect that it might be Andrew and not Celine who was not my mother-in-law's biological child because the Devadas were strategically steering me in that direction. Even Dolly had said that

Aunty Margaret knew of the nine children being born. Just by chance, I met Aunty Margaret's daughter and asked, "Would your mum tell me the truth?" Her response was a silent confident yes. I was not being underhanded, but the Devadas were being secretive, and my anxiety had peaked. I had to find out the truth. Aunty Margaret only mentioned Andrew's missing birth certificate. She did not really know who which child was not her sister's child. This was one vital piece of information that you really do not want to lose. It was at this point that I considered that quite possibly that my mother-in-law was not my mother-in-law. Where was the birth certificate? This led to a dead end and was a waste of time. No one had the courage to tell me the truth; they too were afraid and backtracked. I confronted Andrew and he swore on his mother's grave and on his father's grave and on his son's life that my mother-in-law was his biological mother. This meant nothing to me. The discrepancy between this statement and the different scenarios being played out only meant that he was lying.

I thought the best way to cope was to put on my headphones at Stephen's house, but then I removed them. I had to listen and had to protect myself. It was indeed strange; I saw my in-laws plot to keep their family secrets right before my eyes. Now I understood how disabled people felt when people talked around them almost as if they did not exist, didn't understand. *Baloney!* I was not mentally delayed or challenged. Andrew, who was overly protective of me, was now a ringleader. Mental illness does not mean you lose your judgment and rationality. There was nothing wrong with my hearing. I was scared and afraid that, just maybe, the illness was progressively getting worse and that I was becoming my brother. Was I hearing voices? Did what I see and hear really happen?

Andrew and Stephen tried to contain the secret and use the excuse of my diagnoses. Instinctively and quite perceptively, I knew that my husband was attempting to manipulate me, to play emotional games with me.

One evening, I had bought a present for my niece and then taken it to Johanna's house. There, I saw the family gathered. The family took some enjoyment in my discomfort. His mother would call him a dog for letting the cat out of the bag about Celine not being her biological child.

Stephen's family came from Toronto and stayed with Andrew. At the foot of the stairs, Stephen made a deliberate slip. "So you met my undercover brother?" he said. And Andrew started laughing. In so many ways, he was undercover. I did not say anything. I merely filed this scenario away in the back of my mind. It would be used as evidence to substantiate my final decision and push me on a quest to find the truth for my son. I wanted to know if others would be equally supportive of my quest, and when I researched, I found a law that supported my right of access on behalf of my child. *Surely my request is not unreasonable.* But even without the man-made law, I knew I was within my parameters as a mother to request such information on behalf of my son.

The family was systematically and manipulatively attempting to make me go crazy. Andrew insisted I was imagining things. Other family members perpetrated the game playing and constant abuse. I was afraid – afraid of knowing too much – because here was a family who guarded its secrets and was going to great lengths to keep the secrets, whatever the consequence. It was very scary, a horror movie happening in real life, where people felt the need to maintain lies because (1) they loved their father and (2) they wanted the respectability of perfection. The family – a family who was not so keen on dealing with the truth because truth hurt – was censoring its own senses.

In the end, we all lie to ourselves. I saw the signs but ignored them. For most of the twelve years of my marriage, I was completely caught up in trying to be "true-blue" Sri Lankan; trying so hard to fit in that I was actually daydreaming; and, more importantly, trying to please my husband.

I kept asking Andrew, "Who is Kumar's grandmother?" He ignored my pleas for truth and continued his lies. Truth, for me, is the only thing that protects you. When you tell the truth, you are being fair to another person. I kept on like a broken record. "Who is Kumar's grandmother?"

The family went into overdrive, with elaborate plots and twists to cover up the story. When it was revealed that Aunty Margaret knew the story, they had to strategically invite Aunty Margaret and her husband to Quebec to Johanna's house.

The extended family appeared at Johanna's house for the evening dinner. Some of the mother's children were present, and they wanted a family photo. The family gathered in the living room to have the family photo, and Andrew stood in the hallway, the pathway to the living room. Celine went to sit with the clan, and Andrew stayed behind in the hallway. Alfred, Andrew's younger brother, beckoned his brother to come into the photo, suggestively, as if he was not really the mother's biological son. With the gesture of inclusion, Andrew came to sit in the family photo. And I noticed Alfred's wife smile. The games did not stop here. And though I wished they would stop, I had to fight for myself and my child.

I waited and waited. I knew the truth would reveal itself in the end. Time was the continuum that changes everything, even how we viewed the past. Time, I knew, would let slip the truth.

I stepped out for my son's First Holy Communion. Stephen was there again with his wife, Dolly, who was forced to borrow clothes from my sister-in-law. She had forgotten to bring her own dressy clothes, but if she had Andrew as a husband, she would have been assured of a dressy wardrobe in her suitcase.

The priest who was celebrating the Mass and introducing the little ones there for their First Holy Communion asked, "Will the mothers and grandmothers please come to the front and get the final blessing."

I looked at my mother-in-law and smiled, with a glance that whispered, "Well you are the only grandmother he knows. Let's go up."

Andrew held his own mother back with his arm on her, forcing her to sit down. He forbade her to go up, and Celine, perched on the edge of her seat, looked at me as I, in turn, watched her. It was a roundabout way of implying that the woman I knew as my mother-in-law was not Andrew's biological mother. I, clueless, walked into the circle with my mother-in-law and received the priest's blessings. Andrew sat behind.

Back home, I would wait for my mother-in-law to go to sleep. Then I would go downstairs into the family room and beg Andrew for the truth, if only for my mental health, so I could end my nightmare. I could not understand the in-laws were doing this to me. He would merely provoke me. My eyes were weird or starry-eyed, glazed over like a panther's, fear visible on my face. Andrew saw this as an opportunity to reiterate and bang on: "You are schizo-affective."

Andrew said, "I am going to video you, and I will take it to the counsellor, and he will see how crazy you are."

When I spoke to my counsellor, he merely said, "That won't be necessary."

I fell for Andrew's deliberate taunts and rose to the bait and got angrier and angrier. Now I wanted to say, rent *Gaslight*; it would be a cheaper way for Andrew to see how the dark side of human nature could reside as a life form. I identified with Ingrid Bergman's character, who shared my fears.

My single home, on a slope with lovely cedar trees as a fence and the park in front, now become a cage. I sought to fight for myself without any support. It was not an even fight – a whole clan on one side and me alone on the other. My sister-in-law, Jessie, Alfred's wife, tried to tell the others that what they were doing was wrong. But that was the extent to which her voice could go. She was silenced by Andrew and his family and went with their flow – one wrong supported by a family. Wasn't it strange that even though Jessie told the others that what they were doing was wrong, she herself did not reveal the truth, and she would silence Dolly when she wanted to say the truth But everyone can talk to a stranger, the disinterested for whom the information has no value. No one told me the truth.

Andrew continually harped about a mentally ill wife who was badgering him incessantly and how he had to care for me. For a depressed wife, I did pretty well. Was I really that sick? Generally, I feared that he was convincing an expert and that I was losing credibility.

I thought I would tape their conversations, and I bought a voice-activated recorder and put it beside my mother-in-law's bed. I hoped the recordings would reveal something that I could use to say that I was not crazy and I would stop being so distracted. They were onto my game plan and now moved their conversations into the garage. I was going to capture the truth, and no amount of lying would exonerate them.

I rarely slept in my house. I kept wide awake in the silence of the night, only to be woken by the chatter of long-distance phone calls from Toronto, from Stephen to his mother. The family was assessing what to do next. They had to have a unanimous vote.

Still, surprisingly, it was not loud-mouthed Andrew who had the majority vote as everyone had initially thought. It was Alfred who steered the family, along with Celine. I heard a telling conversation when my mother-in-law repeated what Alfred had said. "Keep the secret. It does not matter if she gets ill; we will take her to the hospital." This sent shock waves through me. Now I knew they didn't care about me.

One night, it became too much for me, with my mother-in-law lifting her bosom and repeating the same lie – "I breastfed ten." I decided to leave my house.

I parked outside a church on the main road and cried. I couldn't remember ever feeling so hurt, so wronged; I tried to find a hotel to stay in for the night, if only for a peaceful night's rest, but there were none nearby.

I returned home, and neither Andrew nor my mother-in-law stirred to see if I was okay. They were desensitised to my pain. I suspected they knew I had no place to go.

Another night, I tried to pack my bags and take Kumar with me, but Andrew forbade it. I could leave alone but not with Kumar. I stayed. I could not sleep; I yearned for a deep sleep. I wanted to AWOL but not without my son.

I could not explain the motivating drive to find the truth when so clearly the family had something to hide and wanted desperately to hide it. Initially I had thought I was helping and doing everything for some imposter. Perhaps, Kumar's real grandmother needed to be found and cared for. What if Kumar's real grandmother was a low caste person or had some messed-up genetic illness that was passed from generation to generation? I had my own messed-up genes.

When Kumar lost his tooth, my mother-in-law advised me to freeze the tooth for stem cell regeneration should Kumar be orphaned. I promptly went with the missing tooth and put it in a bag and in the freezer. She and Andrew smiled. Maybe it was curiosity or something deeper that drove me to find the truth. Or perhaps it was a defence against the allegations that I was a "crazy bitch".

I decided that, whether it was Andrew or his younger sister, Celine, who was not biologically related to their mother, I was going to find out the truth, the scientific truth. I waited and waited, and one day, Andrew, while slicing beef to make a curry, cut his finger and used a tissue to stop the bleeding by wrapping it around the wound. Later he threw it into the garbage, unaware that I was planning to find out the truth. I fished out the bloodied tissue and placed it in a Ziploc bag. Then I took my mother-in-law's toothbrush and put this in another Ziploc bag, labelling both samples. I sent both to a company called Easy DNA, paying around $600 to find the scientific truth – the truth that would give me peace of mind.

I waited for the weeks to pass and then received the email confirmation and test result from Easy DNA. I opened the email slowly and carefully. Finally the truth was here; I hoped that what I read in the email would prove that my mother-in-law was not Andrew's mother. This would be final evidence to substantiate my belief.

It was a case of mistaken identity; as soon as I read the email, I realized it was Celine who my mother-in-law had not given birth to.

The DNA test was positive, and I was confused and dumbfounded. My mother-in-law was Andrew's mother. Why would you steer someone to believe that your mother was not your mother? Whether Celine wanted to hide her identity or the family wanted to protect their father, it was a mess. I could not understand their deception because I had my own niece who was clearly not a blood relative, a parallel life situation.

My niece was white child from Argentina, who grew up in a sea of brown faces. Lydia, a blonde blue-eyed baby in nappies was family. She learnt to eat rice and curry by hand like the rest of the family. I supposed, in our family, we could not very well pass Lydia off as our own biological family member.

I was disappointed with my in-laws, who, as bystanders, had not told me the truth. By their silence, they had participated in and condoned what the others were doing and had overlooked my need; by their silence, they had become culpable.

Even Andrew had refused my pleas for truth on numerous occasions. "Why are you doing this to me?" I would beg. "At least admit that you said what you said to me."

He would ring and talk to me at work but rebuffed my claims that he'd steered me to believe that Kumar's grandmother was not his biological grandmother. He would scream at me and shout that I had imagined the conversations between the various members of his family and and misheard and that my Tamil was not good enough to understand. This was laughable because I had heard everything in English.

My husband was so convincing – and he wanted me to believe that I was very ill – that I started to believe the brainwashing and would wear headphones to silence the talk. Only I would eventually take the headsets off and listen. It was not just Andrew; it was the entire extended family who colluded to play mind games with me, and the movie played in front of me. I watched and listened to their conversations and could not understand why they thought it impossible that I could hear every word. Not just one person was involved; therefore, the brainwashing that I was *that* ill was beginning to be believable.

I knew that you needed truth and trust in order to navigate in the world. I thought I was slowly becoming my brother or my sister, and I was afraid – afraid that, if I went to hospital, I would have ECG treatments and come out a vegetable and that I would be disabled by my mental illness. How, if that were to happen, could I be there for my son? Andrew would have thrown away the key and left me there.

My fears were real. I blocked the talk, but it was hard not to listen, hard because I had to listen to the family plot against me, plot to keep their secrets. Even when I went to my bed to sleep, I kept awake. And once, when Andrew came upstairs to see if I was awake, I kept my body stiff and feigned a deep sleep, closed my eyes, and hushed my breathing – nature's way of playing dead. I had to listen in order to protect myself. I would constantly look at my nails, as if this allowed free reign of my thoughts. It was a habit I acquired as a child.

My vision of my world became blurred, and I doubted myself. I remembered the family home movie night at Alfred's house when we had watched *Shutter Island* and had my own movie night, now knowing their Achilles heel. I wanted them to feel the pain I had experienced, to feel the brunt of a cruel intention. I found a movie at Blockbusters about different types of mothers – some who had adopted their children, some who were abusive mothers, and some who died in childbirth.

I played the movie, and Andrew tried to stand in front of the TV to block his mother from viewing it. She insisted and watched the entire movie. Tough as nails, she stayed. She was hardened by the road, the years of supporting her husband and being loyal only to him. She brainwashed the entire family; loyalty to the family was all that mattered. It was not the difference between right and wrong that she upheld but the family bond. Perhaps the dark and sinister secrets were the strangulating stronghold.

Andrew retaliated with another movie when my friend Bethany came for a visit to Canada. He played a movie about single lonely middle-aged women who had only the company of dogs or cats and were alone at Christmas without any family. The main character in the movie, the lonely duck, was an unwelcome tagalong at family gatherings. Celine accidentally walked in and stayed to watch but left early.

I believed in truth and honesty, but I could not confront the family because they would yet again lie and say, "Where did you get that idea from? What utter disrespect to say that my mother was not my real mother." When the truth of the manipulation was revealed, I, like Ingrid Bergman's character in *Gaslight*, wanted to scream at Andrew, "I hate and despise you and everything you stand for and did to me."

A few weeks later, I revealed what I had done – sending samples to Easy DNA. It was not an illegal act. The right of access of the child supported my claim for the truth, and I had every right to use the toothbrush and tissue with the blood, as I'd found both items in my own home.

I was confused and now started playing my own games with my husband and his family. I lit a candle in church for my mother-in-law. I was unexpectedly comforted, knowing that she actually was Kumar's biological grandmother. In couple's counselling, I asked if the counsellor would want to know the truth. I asked him to put himself in the place of Kumar as an adult and asked, "Would it be important to you?" He merely nodded his agreement.

The truth of the maternity was revealed and proven by the DNA; Andrew was actually my mother-in-law's son. I felt I had failed a test of God. In my own family, I could not very well hide a white child from Argentina, my niece Lydia; her race was obviously a dead giveaway. No explanations necessary. I was sad that Celine felt the necessity to hide her identity while her brother played mind games because I remembered the girl in dungarees and T-shirt in the early days of my marriage, a soufflé-fragile youngster, a butterfly yet to bloom.

Celine had been raised by my mother-in-law as her own child, and she had received much the same treatment as the rest of the children had. Celine had allowed the emotional and mental abuse to continue. She and Andrew had a right to privacy, but neither had a right to abuse me because of it.

I knew, whoever Celine accepted as her mother, be it my mother-in-law or her biological mother, Celine should have been told to go to her room and had her privileges taken away, given the petulant child she was allowing herself to be. She'd held the entire family hostage because of jealousy of me. To be blinded by jealousy and to capitalise on it as an opportunity to hurt me did not make sense.

Unfortunately, it was not only me who'd been damaged but Andrew as well. Celine had allowed the family to sit on the cross for far too long, disregarding the pain caused to her brother, me, and my son. Celine knew the cross, having carried it before – her own inner depression. How she'd allowed herself to permit this was incomprehensible.

Celine confessed her own story to at least seven others. She wielded power in the form of control of information; it wasn't the protection of her mother that she sought. The family that had supported her had also supported her jealousy for their own reasons, a culmination of jumping on the bandwagon. How easily jealousy ruled the roost and became the leader and how swiftly the followers lost their own voice and rights as they followed suit. In the end, we are only accountable for our own actions.

Jealousy is a universal emotion, like greed, selfishness, and vanity. My brothers were often jealous of me, and their jealousy interfered with their relationship with me. I was envious of my sister and jealous at times. I resented the ease with which Hamza fitted into her age, the clothes, and the holidays and her model looks. At some point, I knew that my journey was meant to be a different one and that, like apples and pears, I could not compare myself and my sister. While looking at the highlights of Hamza's life, I failed to see the highlights in my own life.

I was slightly flattered that a wallflower and misfit would warrant such attention. But when I looked back at everything, as when I'd surveyed the car accident scene and my old green Camry, I was saddened. I had given my in-laws so many chances to avoid the final straw that broke the camel's back.

It does not matter that we fall and have to go back and relearn the lesson because it is a journey. Papa said, "You can only help them when they fall." Both I and Celine had failed a test, a test set by the universe. A family of God needs no bloodline.

🦋 🦋 🦋

In among all this commotion, Andrew was trying to tell me something and took me to a restaurant of a different kind.

Shush, It's a Secret

*N*ow, my dear readers you would like to know the juicy tabloid details of who let the cat out of the bag and who actually affirmed the mental, sexual, and physical abuse. But even in the story one needs to protect the characters. If the reader or the characters wanted the pretext of a deluded wife with an overactive imagination, then so be it. Truth lies between the gaps of the pages, God, and the participating parties. The code of secrecy is necessary for a story of such a nature.

Alfred was naive in his own way because, if he felt that his wife and others were not talking, then he was remiss in his thinking.

"A secret is never a secret," Papa said. "If you tell one person, at least five people know." Papa was just as remiss in not telling me that a secret is distributed; five times five equals twenty-five people. The spread of Chinese whispers and the Sri Lankan telegram of oral tradition is all that is needed. When a story leaves one mouth as an apple, it is received, by ear, as a pear. All the various add-ons and omissions make the story even more colourful. Yes I talked, *but* I talked about the family attempting to convince me that I was both my brother and sister rolled into one.

The system that colludes to such an extent to have someone silenced is scary; I was manipulated into believing I was mentally delusional, and I felt threatened when Andrew blew out my tyre. I was afraid, and my heart was pounding; my stomach was somersaulting, and I could not eat. The stress was too great. I was always vigilant and alert. Should these characters stumble upon this book, I did not reveal what I knew, if anything. My rationale was this – why should I tell them what God already knows?

I did not want to hear anymore. To carry the burden of knowing meant that I needed to do something. I no longer wanted to participate with silence. To do so meant I condoned and accepted the abuse and that I was a bystander to someone else's pain. I discovered a French philosopher, Foucault, and understood that information is valorised, circulated, and distributed as a power tool. *Isn't it strange how things make no sense at all until you have a personal experience?*

Information now, I had come to understand could be manipulated to heal, empower, humitalte degrade or uplift.

One Last Attempt: Should I Stay or Go?

I was not assertive enough to choose my own style in the house. Andrew chose every piece of furniture, until one day, I went and bought some Levelor blinds and a red quilt for my bed.

How can I change my relationship? I kept asking myself. *I am just not happy the way it's going.* I decided to take action, to take steps to see if I could improve my relationship, instead of moving furniture or buying blinds.

I found a counsellor who was an expert in his field. It did seem an odd profession, where you are required to spend an hour sitting and listening to some stranger spieling about the blah-blah-blah of what is going on in life. Dr Gilbert came highly recommended. When I went into his small office with soft lighting and wall-to-wall bookcases filled with heavy material, I was in awe of the integrity of study, a humbling experience. It was quite impressive really that he studied so intensively, narrowing the scope to become an expert. I faced a tall slim man who appeared quite unassuming. In many respects, he was a dead ringer for Jesus, or perhaps it was the profession that made me think of this archetype.

A session with the counsellor felt more like being in confession; you had to trust him, even though you did not know him. Instead of running the list of sins, I ran a list of life events, in the hope that Dr Gilbert would miraculously heal my life and set the compass on a different direction. I wanted to ask my counsellor, "Now that you know everything, what should I do?"

Initially, I felt that the one-hour session was a complete waste of time because Dr Gilbert was just listening to my story. At some point, he must have been bored.

I felt blessed, though, because Dr Gilbert a clinical psychologist had specialized in studying schizophrenia. He had a vast number of years' experience and was definitely nobody's fool. I felt comforted. My in-laws would find it very hard to pull the wool over his eyes.

During the first three sessions, Dr Gilbert kindly offered to give me some kind of psychiatric evaluation. There were two questionnaires to complete. One was the diagnostic questionnaire-4 (PDQ-4), and the other was the Minnesota Multiphasic Personality Inventory. These tests were designed to determine my mental health status and to see if the diagnoses I'd been given were accurate.

I apprehensively filled out the questionnaire and left it with Dr Gilbert. I was anxious about what the results would reveal. But felt I could have the closure I needed, especially with so much turmoil going on in my life. The week was long – waiting, waiting, and waiting:

When I next returned for a session, I was anxious. Dr Gilbert went over the results with me.

"You are not schizo-affective," he told me. "You are depressed. You are avoidant – dependant and depressed."

I really did not know what that meant. "What does that mean," I asked him.

Dr Gilbert explained, "You do not like confrontations and will avoid them. You find it hard to have close meaningful relationships." *Who would after everything I have been through.*

I now understood myself better. I also rationalized that if your "home" life was spent avoiding situations where what you said or did might provoke the other's temper, obviously you would naturally become more avoidant in time. If I was dependant, it was because I was being steered to believe that I was incapable and needed my husband. Andrew was treating me like a child and telling everyone that he loved me like a daughter.

What Dr Gilbert had discussed about the tests was a relief. At this point, I realised that what I had lived with all these years had taken its toll mentally. I breathed a sigh of relief to learn that the label my in-laws had been attempting to force me to accept was unhelpful and did not apply. I fell within the parameters of average scoring, and I was not hearing voices. I wondered how psychiatrists ever made decisions without considering their clients' stress factors and the environment that contributed to a person going "off radar". Dr Gilbert had explained that the Minnesota Multiphasic Personality Inventory was a ruler and that everyone would fall somewhere on its spectrum. I pondered whether, if these tests were administered more and more often, more and more people would be labelled "abnormal" and the rates of Obsessive Compulsive Disorder, schizo, SAD, paranoia, manic depressive, borderline personality and other diagnosable diseases would go up among the population. I considered all these things negative placebos or unhelpful labels that did not pay attention to the stressful environments that *caused* a person to test higher on the "ruler". They were talking about me being crazy when his family has gone mad.

During my sessions with Dr Gilbert, he slowly helped me began to realise that the white picket fence; single home; and mother, father, and child scenario was definitely not going to work for me. I expected something else. I was disappointed. Neither Andrew nor I wanted to retire with each other. Andrew never asked me if I was ever happy. He only espoused, "I could never retire with you." There were two people in this marriage. It was quite scary when I was alone in Canada with no family support. I felt dispersed, isolated, and alone.

Andrew attended only three sessions of marriage counselling. After the first session, the counsellor did remark that Andrew was an angry man. *Thank God, you see that too!* I thought. Andrew came out of the first counselling session, and in his face, I saw a beam of delight. It was as if the hour-long venting had done him some good. The explosive anger was offering only temporary relief. He said, "I feel better now."

I got to witness Andrew shooting fire again, but now the episodes were more frequent and the intensity did not wane. As usual, the longstanding projection was that Andrew was dealing with a sick wife, but thankfully, the counsellor did not agree.

His anger was one of the reasons I had succumbed to a state emergency; I could feel myself holding my breath and the uncomfortable way my stomach churned. His anger wasn't the only contributing factor; my desire to be equal to my new family had also played a part in creating a "misfit". I had sought their approval and cared what they thought of me. Andrew had been abused mentally and physically. I was finally able to piece together why I'd had such a nightmare of a marriage. I was living with a wounded and angry man, whose abuse had left deep within him an inner turmoil. The family had told Andrew not to go to therapy because our counsellor, a clinical psychologist, had specialised in studying schizophrenia.

I was always sensitive to people's opinion of me, as I was trying to carve a place for myself outside of stereotypes.

In my naivety, I assumed that my decline into depression was to blame for the demise of my relationship and that Andrew could not cope with a mentally ill wife. I came to this assumption because I trusted Andrew's judgment, loved him, and thought I could count on him. He had said, "You can trust me. I am your husband." He blamed my illness for his anger. On a scale of one to ten, when assessing my own mental state, I knew that I was nowhere near ten. I had lived with my brother and sister and knew the distinction and disparity between a severely mentally ill person and a depressed person.

It was comforting to know that I was not delusional; imagining voices and unreal stories was not really in me. It was in counselling that I discovered that the type of irrational unprovoked anger in Andrew had existed before my marriage and that Andrew was a victim long before I ever fell ill. This was just an excuse, a cover-up for the real reason for his anger and the continual lies – a deflection and projection to excuse his own temper. I was desensitised towards that anger; I had lived the drama of my own family. He was the proverbial pot calling the kettle black.

Ammah in Canada

mmah's last visit to Canada was tinged with the dark side of life. Ammah was forced to listen to comments like, "Your sons are worthless bums," and, "You will go to purgatory for where your son is today; it is your fault." It was my mother-in-law who spoke these words. This was another relationship that caused me angst – the competition of the mothers, similar in vein to the battle for head of the family between Balram and Andrew. I had to sit and watch Ammah's discomfort and watch her maintain the same steadfast calm, never flinching to show her pain. In the eyes of my mother-in-law, she was standing up for me, espousing all the ways Ammah had not been there in my life to help me. Ammah did not ring me enough, Ammah did not visit me enough, Ammah did not come after I had Kumar to help me. My mother-in-law wanted me to only see everything she did for me in the last twelve years of my life.

Ammah and my mother-in-law together in the house was not a recipe for a good mix. This was another thorny relationship – like Balram and Andrew's – that did not make things easy for me. Ammah was vulnerable, and my mother-in-law knew this and would torment her. However, my mother-in-law would make sure Ammah ate during the day whenever I was at work. She was an octogenarian who would teach Ammah how to train her mind by using the rosary beads and reciting aspirations by rote to instil in her a conversion from weakness to strength. She took Ammah to churches and prayer meetings with the nuns, which was a highlight for Ammah.

When I took them both to the restaurant, my mother-in-law would say about Ammah, "She says she does not want food and then finishes it," almost as if she was a greedy child.

112

Ammah was always good at forgiving and simple in thinking. "You can change some things, and you have to live with others," she would say to me. "One day, you might need forgiveness."

This did not make sense to me. I asked my mother, "Ammah, what if one day, twelve years into your marriage, Papa revealed something to you, say a secret you hadn't known, how would you feel? Would you forgive?"

It was the only time Ammah stayed silent. She would usually defend Andrew and say, "Whatever happened to you? You used to be an angel, not so angry." I can only understand my change to a volatile person because of the abuse. I had a right to be angry about the years of torment, of living with an angry man.

I lashed out, shooting fire, combating fire with fire, and snarling verbally like a trapped animal without empathy and remorse. My husband and his family would always bad-mouth my family, saying that my brothers were worthless bums and my mother was stupid and could not see that she was being used. Most families expect that the bloodline gives a freehand; we use and abuse those closest to us, feeling like we're entitled to do so simply because we are brothers, sisters, mother, and father. It is a bond that only the bloodline seems to understand. What goes on between one daughter and a mother only they understand; each relationship is different from the other.

I hated the fact that I had to leave Ammah at home, but I had to go to work. Ammah wanted to go back to London, and I waved goodbye to her at the airport and said, "I don't know when I'll see you again."

Ammah said, "Of course you're going to see me again. I'm doing so much better now."

When I received the phone call telling me that Ammah was going for hip surgery, I rang Andrew and he told me to wait and see. "She just went back, wait and see what happens to her." I knew Andrew could make Papa look generous.

I screamed at the phone and said, "Balram said come home now. I'm going."

I booked my flights and started packing.

Ammah had died before I could make it back. I knew that Ammah had suffered emotional abuse at Andrew's house – a by-product of the games Andrew's family played was that civilians suffered and paid the price. At the airport, I looked at Andrew and said, "You let my mother think I was crazy." If a brown man could go white, he sure looked pale as the blood drained from his face.

When Ammah died, though I was rendered powerless and was not there at her bedside, I found a release, and I cried and cried, partly for Ammah but partly for myself – for all that I had undergone during my life in Canada. Everyone thought Ammah could do anything. If someone asked her for her prayers, she would not only pray but would be on the phone to call the London Healing Mission and others.

Ammah travelled wherever she could to find Jesus and Mary, so when the time came for my passing, the priest in Brook Green Church said that Ammah saw Jesus when the priest was celebrating Mass. Everyone believed it. Ammah wouldn't lie; she was very devoted to her prayers.

At Ammah's funeral, I cried on Kaneswari's shoulder, partly because I knew she loved Ammah and partly as a release for everything I had gone through. I knew that, as a Malaysian Tamil in the community, she would understand my journey more so than my siblings.

When it came time to clean out Ammah's belongings, Hamza found in Ammah's handbag a note with each of her children's name. Next to each name were a wish and a prayer for his or her life. Next to my name, Ammah's prayer was that I no longer be depressed and be happy.

There was also a letter from Papa, which read, "My darling wife, I have spent \$1,500 and had to give my brother Manick \$700 for the funeral expenses. Please take care of the children." Strangely, the aerogramme, which was both letter and envelope, contained only a few lines; Papa was a man of few words even in writing.

After Ammah's death, the family had a symbolic cataract eye surgery. We could not keep her with us forever, and though life is a teacher, Ammah's death was a teacher and a miracle. We had all taken her life for granted, as if she had all the time in the world.

The three directions of the fountain were symbolic of the three mothers – Ammah, my mother, the non-confrontational fool who allowed things to happen to her; me, the naive and trusting fool, educated but gullible; and my mother-in-law, the misguided and deluded fool. These mothers facing opposite directions were caught in our own "sense of time", and we protected ourselves with our own lies – a censor of the senses. None of these breeds of woman could understand the decisions or desires of the other but somehow had to come to terms with the decision of the others. Each, trapped by her sense of time in her continuum of life, was only responsible for her own decision.

The Visit:
The Truth Revealed

The light bulb only flashed when I visited a spiritualist church in London, after Ammah's death and funeral. I was late for my appointment, walking up and down trying to find the place. I had been going from one psychic to another, from one spiritualist to another to find out what I should do with my life. I went to another church and then had to retrace my steps, and then I finally found a taxi. It was getting too late, and I might miss my appointment.

Inside, I met a white woman in her early sixties with permed curly hair. I had often been told I was a fool and gave away too much information, so I said, "Can I have a piece of paper? And can you tell me everything Ammah wants me to know."

I wanted to connect with Ammah, to find out what she had to say. Ammah had messages for everyone.

Then Jenny, the spiritualist, told me, "You do know he is a homosexual. And you should know; you were married to him."

And yes it finally made sense – the lack of intimacy, no kissing, the avoidance of emotional contact, and the stress he put on me so that he could play football with the boys. The taxi driver would say, "A good-looking woman like you, and he wants to play soccer."

He never really kissed me during our marriage and would only make love now and again, using the excuse that I was sick. I assumed it was because he had a science background. He was an engineer; he must have been afraid of germs passing when you kiss. I never thought it was because he didn't ever feel close to me and had never really wanted or been able to give me the closeness I desired. More importantly, he'd never really loved me.

"Was he abused?" I asked the psychic.

After listening to the other side, the psychic replied, "Yes, mentally and physically."

Wow, now all the pennies fell into place. I looked back, and all the clues were there. He didn't want a relationship with me.

I wanted to know if my mother would be okay with me getting out of my marriage.

Jenny told me, "She has seen everything from heaven, and she is saying to focus on your freedom and to go back and look after your son."

"What about Papa? How does he feel about the house being sold?"

The psychic listened and replied, "He doesn't need it where he is."

I understood that, on the other side, Fathima's earrings, Papa's house, and my father-in-law's honour were only good for the living. But somehow, "honour" only impeded the love of God; it was a false adoration. I now understood that the false God was not another faith. But it could be a bad relationship, the forced love of a parent, the ambitions of the parents, enslaving wife and enslaving husband. What is the point of staying in a marriage if being in that partnership requires us to go against our own grain – to deny that which makes up our inner self?

Now all the jigsaw pieces fitted in place. A Tamil homosexual and a coconut was not *West Side Story*. I felt like a prize fool. I had believed I had something in my marriage, but it turned out to be this nothingness, emptiness, and there I was – stuck with a fool's gold. If only I could erase my memory and forgive and let go.

The train ride back to Hamza's place was filled with a racing mind; only this time, I was coming to terms with what Jenny had told me.

The Getaway

After Ammah's funeral in England, I felt the pull of my son, Kumar. I called to talk to him, and Kumar said, "You can stay, Mum. We are fine."

I knew the time had come to go back and face my life. Still not knowing what I was going to do, I flew back to Canada. Andrew didn't come to the airport, under the pretext of working on call as a support engineer. I took a taxi home. Immediately, my mother-in-law said, "He was fine until you showed up, and now he is all anxious again."

"What would you expect from someone who has been lying to his wife?" I responded.

Celine came to my house. I was already in the car, reversing down the slope for an exit. I merely glanced at Celine, and neither of us spoke. Celine just looked back and walked up to the front door. There seemed no point in talking now. Ammah had died thinking that I was as sick as my sister and brother. Ammah was already dying when she'd come to Canada. I said to Andrew, "The one thing no one counted on is how much I love my mother." It was one of the reasons I could no longer stay.

My eldest sister-in-law, Johanna, came round, and the same lies continued. "If she doesn't ask anything, just keep quiet," she instructed her mother. She was always good at teaching her mother to suck eggs.

I was motivated by unsurpassed adrenalin that charged me, and I set the wheels to get out of my marriage in motion. This was the final straw; the continual lies and disregard of the pain caused all round was the act that broke all bonds. I didn't consider the "how" or the "when" or whether I could do it. The spark had been ignited.

I confronted Andrew about his sexuality, saying with accusation in my tone, "You are a homosexual."

All he said was, "And now you are questioning my sexuality; you are crazy."

I was angry about the deception, hurt that I had wasted so many years based on a lie. It was only later that I would regret these words, because I had compounded the hurt. Suddenly, my marriage flashed before my eyes and everything made sense. "If only you had told me the truth, I would have given you your life back years ago. And I would have had my own life."

Johanna and her husband came to the house, and again, I could not sleep. Every breath they took seemed to suggest that Andrew should not want me because I fed my child burgers.

At the door, I told them both, "It was my twelve years of marriage that have gone down the pan."

Twelve wasted and stolen years.

I knew Johanna and her husband were there for Andrew, and if anyone came to visit me it was a *feigned* support. They came well-rehearsed with lines to convince me that Celine was actually a C-section. I understood that they were really covering up the fact, or attempting one last ditch attempt to convince me before I left the family fold. They wanted to protect the information. This was their reason for dredging up Celine's maternity. Still they continued and it was exasperating and destabilising.

From Jenny's voice in England on the other the end of the phone, I drew strength and broke away from Andrew's control. I went with my friend Nikki and bought a car, a hybrid green Camry. I still was not sure of my decision, I wanted to help Andrew and we sat in the restaurant going over *Am I doing the right thing?*

Andrew was suddenly waking up to the end of the marriage, and he wanted to go to church with me. I could count the times I'd gone to church with him before – we'd gone three times as a family in twelve years.

"It's too late," I said.

We'd only spent two holidays together as a family. On one, we'd gone away to a friend's cottage, and for the duration, Andrew had been bored and restless, craving the entourage. The second holiday was a visit to my family and then my friend in Germany. Andrew had grumbled about having to come to England and then to Germany.

Andrew was not at ease or comfortable around my friends and dragged his feet there. It was a hard chore being with his wife and her friends, and I only understood that it was escapism; he could not live a lie. He was struggling to keep up the charade, and it was destroying him. All the clues, all the signs and I still did not get it. I was educated but dumb.

I told Kumar, my son what I planned to do, and as a child without a filter, he promptly told his father. After that, everything was high adrenalin. Michael, a friend of Andrew's from work and a fellow engineer, and my friend Nasreen from the days when we stayed in the apartment in Greenbank Towers were the only ones willing to witness the end of the marriage.

With all the shouting and fighting going on, neither I nor Andrew saw three little children hiding in the closet until one day, Nasreen's child asked "why is Uncle shouting at Aunty?"

The usual negative accusations were thrown in the air. "Your family is all about divorces," Andrew said. And later, he said, "My brother said you are a bitch for doing this to Kumar and me."

I could live with the dumbass comments; I was, after all, doing something out of the ordinary and out of normalcy. I had already lived with cruelty long enough to know that it existed, though I could never understand it.

Michael recommended a mediator to both of us. The mediator was a tubby guy wearing a Swiss Alps Benetton woolly cardigan. He had overgrown hair, and he also had a PhD in clinical psychology. He espoused that there is no such thing as "dis-ease" or "diag-noses". Andrew arrived early to let the mediator know that his wife was "schizoaffective" and that he was looking after her. At the first session, more anger brewed and Andrew said he wanted the marriage to work. It was too late. He wanted it to work for all the wrong reasons.

The mediator said, "Are you hearing her? She doesn't want to get back with you." Co-parenting was going to be tough. The verbal slinging match continued; the usual old stories were being dredged up as Andrew tried to convince the mediator that I had dreamed up the story of Celine maternity. It was a form of social abuse, that Andrew went around telling everyone that I was delusional. The reason I brought this up was to show that I was not ill as he made me appear. And he kept saying, "She is schizo-affective." The mediator was the second expert who'd witnessed Andrew's anger. He was so upset at his outburst that he was afraid to see him again at the next session. His only advice to me was to get out quickly "before he convinces you that you need a straitjacket and you end up marching yourself into Douglas Hospital, Quebec."

I was forced to find a family lawyer. He was a great negotiator and calmly put the entire thing together. I started looking at grapevine, a Web site where home buyers and sellers could view or place ads. I needed to find a house within my means.

At work, he was still harassing me but now he sent me a photo of a woman with a black eye and the reason she got the black eye was because she did not cook the rice properly. I was not sure why he sent this to me. He probably wanted to intimidate me or to challenge me on the point of my abuse. I suspect, even abusers need educating about what constitutes an abuse and that there are different types.

Luckily, I found a townhouse and befriended the seller. The seller was living there after her own separation, and she was an advocate of living in the moment and letting go of the past. She helped me with the status of certificate and offered to move out early so that I could begin my life again and to avoid the further damaging of mind games.

I had loved my in-laws, my nephews and nieces, and my years living with them. I had to say goodbye to them, and it was hard and painful. But I knew no other way because old hurts resurfaced afresh with a new glow of immediacy whenever I saw them. I hugged the children and knew no way to explain why I could not be in their lives. They probably wouldn't realise it was the last time they would see me.

I was afraid of getting hurt again and again, so I forced myself to turn my back on the past. Surprisingly though, it was Lydia, my niece in England who would use her voice and presence as a tool against injustice when she came to Canada for a visit. "I do not care if they have a swimming pool; after everything they did to Idhaya, I don't want to go there."

🦋 🦋 🦋

When I went shopping in the mall, strangely, I saw Dr Surgit, my psychiatrist, chatting away with his family. I approached the table where he was sitting with his family eating at the food court.

"How are you?" he asked. "I haven't seen you for a while?"

I told him that I had left and bought a home.

He just absorbed the information.

I said my goodbyes, and as I left, I heard him turn to his family and say, "She is here on her own, without her family support, and her in-laws are not always nice to her." I wondered why he did not lead with my diagnoses.

The Mangled Butterflies

*A*mélie was my French Zumba instructor. She would sit at the passenger side of the vehicle and oozed confidence; she talked incessantly in French to assess my understanding and fluency of the language. She also would explain the rules of the road. She was scared – scared that my expertise on the road was not a match for her. Both she and I often allowed the hour dance lesson to veer off topic.

There were no airs or graces with Amélie. She was a no-nonsense type of person, yet she was kind, gentle, and warm. She was a redheaded butterfly – defensive, vulnerable, and strong. She was wonderfully ethereal, a little mermaid far from home. She would walk to the car, heavily loaded with a black bag that was filled with French books to help me. Only five feet tall and slightly round, she would struggle to lug the bag. She was ambitious and had an actual "bucket list" and was cramming her life with lost opportunities. She had a personality that saw the funny side of the ridiculous and an unreserved infectious giggle that could warm a tragedy. A light-hearted nature and a magnetism of her own were deeply characteristic of Amélie. She was a survivor of abuse, though the pain of her past and what she had endured was never written on her face. Her glass was never half empty; it was always half full. Amélie and I quickly became friends; we bonded in a moment of excruciating emotional plain. I was leaving Andrew.

Amélie was sitting in my house when I was talking to my lawyer, who wanted me to get more assets from Andrew. But I told my lawyer that I did not want stay and divide furniture and bank loans that were not mine. I was on the phone with my lawyer. "I am sitting opposite a woman who left her husband after sixteen years of physical and mental abuse with nothing but the clothes she piled in her car," I told my lawyer. I explained how, when Amélie returned with the police to get the rest of her things, she discovered that her ex-husband had demolished most of the things in her house. She'd had to leave her dog behind, and when she attempted to return to get him, she found that her ex-husband had maliciously put him to sleep.

I glanced at Amélie. I noticed that my friend's eyes had glazed over like a panther's and she was far away now. Amélie had gone to her lawyer, but her settlement was no more than $3,000, and that had been absorbed by lawyer's fees. Many people, including her current partner, would ask her why she'd stayed so long and why she hadn't been able to leave sooner.

I faced the same question. "How could you not know he was a homosexual? Why did you not get out?" I had been sleepwalking for those years, too absorbed in assimilating, in trying to be someone other than a misfit, an oddity.

Amélie confided that her grandfather had sexually abused her. It was only in Douglas Hospital in Quebec that she discovered that she had developed multiple personalities to cope with her abuse. Her childlike screams that were played back to her were unrecognisable to Amélie. Her grandfather would cum in her hand, starting when she was only a year old and push his penis against her pyjamas. He would threaten her as she slept next to her sister and warn her that he would do the same thing to her little sister too.

Amélie later revealed that her grandfather had, in fact, abused three of her cousins in a similar way. Though the four girls shared their stories once, they never spoke about it again. It was a one-time revelation, and after that, the code of secrecy again reared its ugly head.

Through Amélie, I would find many others who had suffered abuse as children. Amélie would answer questions that I knew my in-laws would never answer honestly.

I asked her, "What do you feel about your mother who knowingly left you with your grandfather? She did know that he was an abuser."

Amélie eyes were downcast; she could not answer. Her love of her mother surpassed any issues one could project upon a mother and daughter. Even abused children love their parents.

She helped explain to me why Andrew was so angry. He had been violated physically and mentally.

"How do you feel about your grandfather?"

All Amélie could respond was that he was a very sick man. In her own way, she had come to terms with what had happened to her and rationalised the abuse. She'd never once blamed her mother. I witnessed Amélie's anger towards her father. She would scold him. And when talking about her grandfather, she would scream, cursing him. And turning to her father, she would say, "And I will bury you next to him".

When she was recently diagnosed with ADHD, she joked with God, "And you throw this at me too." To some, Amélie appeared to be a cursed unblessed woman; she had so many crosses to bear. Yet, she was accepting of her crosses and became a champion and a survivor. Despite her many challenges, she sought to give back to women, to uplift their self-esteem; she wanted them to feel beautiful, to feel pampered and cared for.

Amélie, like I, would connect with mediums to find closure with loved ones. We shared a similar sense of humanity that was inclusive. When I met Amélie, I tried to move my hurt aside to understand why my ex-husband had tortured me and why my in-laws had colluded to keep their brother from seeking help and acknowledging his pain.

I finally understood Andrew's outbursts; the family had denied him the voice to address the truth about what had happened to him. I wondered too, how Andrew felt about his own brothers and sisters for suppressing the hurt and pain and blocking his healing process. How must he feel? They believed their own lies and remained deluded. Years living with them meant I had become a mind reader, and I imagined certain individuals advising Andrew. "You don't have to go for counselling just because she tells you," one might say. "Why do you want to come out anyway? You are fifty-three after all," another would counsel.

Ego was another barrier to healing. What was my alternative? Should you let the man rant and rave for another twenty years until he has a heart attack? I could not understand a family system that let someone stay in pain.

Amélie said, by way of an explanation, "He cannot come out, honey. They won't let him."

When they shared their stories, Amélie told me, "Yes, honey, you were abused mentally and emotionally." This was the first time anyone ever told me that what I had undergone was not acceptable, course 101, how I was abused.

Slowly, I recognised that, even though Andrew had the loudest voice and biggest rage, he had no voice for himself.

Amélie also revealed that had I met her a few years back, I would not have liked the person she was – an alcoholic self-abusive person.

Amélie and I made a pact to write our stories – one as the victim of sexual and physical abuse and the other as a victim of emotional and mental abuse. I was clear about the message I wanted to get out there. As victims, I believed, we are responsible and have a duty to seek help so that we do not unwittingly abuse another person. As families of the victims, we need to ensure that healing is possible, not by secrets and lies, but by addressing the problem in a safe environment. That which is done cannot be undone or rewritten, but healing can be possible. Abuse creates primary victims and secondary victims in the cause-and-effect chain of events. If the abused person is left untreated for too long, the damage is irreversible, and without help, casualties will be caught in the unhealthy spider's web.

Andrew was a child stuck in an aging body, with an overinflated self-esteem that hid his own vulnerability, and his release came in unwittingly destroying me and forcing me to march to a tune so different from the essence of myself. The pace was on guard, fast and without rest. I now began to see Andrew as a mangled butterfly.

Andrew's anger had damaged me, and the road from devil to angel towards healing was a slow one. For me, fear had been debilitating and uncontrollable; a foreign entity that had paralysed and blocked me from interacting, setting goals, or starting anything, it had consumed my mind and body. I had little control over my bowel movements and was nervous about the smallest of tasks. Being stressed and in fear meant that I woke up on high adrenalin; I was taut like tight wire and choking on my own speed. My ovaries twanged like a guitar, and I felt a pinching throb on my left side. My irritable gut played its own twisting turmoil inside, and my stomach stretched and contorted in a grimacing way. My stiffness from my arthritis meant extra time in the morning to oil my joints. Inside my body, a horrible discordant symphony played, and it was a hard dance. My insides were mush, my mind filled with apprehension and foreboding of the possibility that I could have a life like my mother's and become carer for a child who could be ill I worried constantly over Kumar's future and whether genetically he too was predisposed to mental illness; it was why I walked on eggshells all the time, it was why I tried so hard to help him early with his learning disability.

I continued to visit my counsellor, Dr Gilbert, and kept him informed of what was happening. When I went to visit him, he would asked, "What do you see?"

"Nothing," was my reply at first.

Then later on, I was able to see only a butterfly. Having one's world turned upside down is quite the rollercoaster. All the lies hurt more than the truth. I did not know anything anymore; I looked at everyone differently. Where do you go from here?

I started to draw for my book, to help with the healing. I wanted to know why it had taken me so long to figure everything out. It was hard to find highlights in my world to keep me warm and fuzzy, to keep me positive.

I felt deceived by the very people I had come to love as my own brothers and sisters, deceived by a community who supported those lies and got away with it. I was stupid to have believed that my "own kind" would not deceive me, a belief I'd nurtured from a child. I had been taught that the outsider was the user. Years wasted on a bad marriage were the slow death of the mockingbird. Hurt, deluded, and broken, I did not know how I was going to pick myself up again.

The Impromptu
Book Review

In my bid to get the book finished, printed, and in circulation, I continued working on it again. I wanted to remember everything and to be finally free of my past. I needed and wanted truth. The mundane and banal existence of work created an opportunity to work after hours on the weeks I did not have Kumar.

One day in May, I printed a copy of my journal, but being trigger-happy, I clicked on the mouse and accidentally printed two copies by mistake. I did not know of my negligence until the next morning, when my boss remarked, "Who has been doing personal work?" He merely handed the journal back to me. I hoped my boss and co-workers would not have read it or circulated the journal.

An impromptu book review was held in my boss's office. Three colleagues – John Digby, the director; Daniella Chase, the deputy director; and Michelle Labelle, an officer – were sitting having lunch at the round table usually used for meetings. They were all three engaged in discussing the content of the book, and I sat at my director's desk typing a work-related material.

Michelle asked, "Why didn't Idhaya's father tell them that he was ill?"

John responded, on my behalf, as if I was absent, "It is because the family had gone through so much. Does anyone else know about her brother?"

John further said, "Do any of you remember the catalogue?" referring to the time Papa showed me the Freeman's catalogue. They too were reminiscing about the times when these were part of the norm of everyday life. And I wanted to say, *What about the typewriter with the carriage return?* But I remained stayed silent.

The analysis did not stop there. As Daniella and Michelle cleared their desks and walked him, I overheard a conversation. They referred to the birthday incident and questioned the validity of my being upset. "Do you think Idhaya was being too sensitive?" asked Danielle. "Maybe her illness made her overreact and exaggerate what happened, the family's intention?"

Michelle responded, "I don't think so because, remember, there was the report from the psychologist that nothing was wrong with her and she is within the parameters of average scoring."

Danielle responded "Yeah, you are right! And don't forget about her husband. Remember, he got their son to blow out the candles to slap the others down."

I was not really glad about the impromptu book review, but it happened. I was glad that they were focussing on my right to be sensitive and whether it was a valid reaction.

I was glad that the impromptu book review was giving everyone an opportunity to analyse the situation of my life. John Digby wanted to know what "drove her crazy". And quite honestly, this was why I had written the book; it was a coming to terms with one's past and letting go. It was a journey to ask two essential questions: (1) What was making Andrew so angry? (2) What events triggered my demise into depression? Was there a correlation between his anger and my depression? Should we not all focus on being happy in life and having a passion.

I remembered my mother-in-law and her list of good deeds; I was keeping my own tally of negative deeds. I was on a quest to find out whether it was one act or a series or a flooding of acts over the years that had taken their toll mentally and physically.

Aside from this impromptu book review, secretly my colleagues were working to get me a promotion. I had earned my right to be in a pool of qualified candidates for such a promotion.

Unfortunately, my own dumbass off-colour comment about my previous boss, Jonathan Drummond, which I'd said in a private conversation, was brought into the public workspace.

I started to look at everyone differently. I paid close attention to what everyone else said about a person; when someone gave verbal narratives about others, it really gave me a sense of who the person talking was. I sometimes was dumb, and other times, I was quite perceptive. I felt that I did not know anyone, especially when I started writing my book and looking at my life.

I got caught making with an off-colour remark, and Jonathan withdrew the offer of the promotion. There was something of the Bridget Jones in my being caught in such a circumstance.

My current boss, John felt bad about the promotion being taken away, and he showed Jonathan my journal to persuade him to reconsider, thereby clinching the deal of the promotion. The off-again promotion then became an on-again promotion. Even the company's vice president wanted to know what was in the book that had changed his mind. I had to keep quiet about the promotion. On the sidelines, I saw my colleagues' good heart and intention in trying to secure the promotion for me. When Jonathan offered me the promotion, I would have to act surprised and not spoil it by saying, "I already knew."

Unfortunately, the book did not deliver what I intended; it created an awakening for the thrill of injury – the same reckless attitude. John was empowered because he became the gatekeeper of the book. Instead of being a deterrent for emotional and mental abuse, the book became the catalyst of the awakening of a false power, and it was compounded with a mob, which in the end, created a similar toxic work environment. They used similar mind games as those used by Andrew and his family to excuse their participation in reading and circulating the book around the office and then finally to Jessie.

John made an incisive comment in reference to Hamza, referring to her as "the prettier younger sister." When I confronted him, he merely brushed this comment off, as if he had not read or known that the book belonged to me. He merely responded, "You know the prettier younger sister is the one at home." He also admitted in passing, "We can do what they did and get away with it." I was perturbed and disillusioned. He was learning something from the book about how to abuse. I was caught off my guard again.

Since Andrew was a closet homosexual and the book referenced the lack of intimacy and sex in my life, John and Maria thought it amusing to sing and dance to the lyrics of "(Can't Get No) Satisfaction" while I sat at my desk. I knew they were having fun at my expense, alluding to the lack of intimacy in my marriage. They made so many inferences that alluded to the fact that they had read my personal book. They did not want to own up to this and I was left out of the circle of readers who read my personal book.

I recalled the autobiographical movie on Abraham Lincoln and his fight to abolish slavery. The means with which he gained votes were bribery and corruption, yet the purity of his intention, the abolition of slavery was the greater good, as it would mean an end of suffering and torture.

Here, I wondered whether the means to the end was justifiable. The journal circulated so the off-the-table promotion became on again? I marvelled at how Maria kept messing things up. She was given courage, with the help of Michelle, who would march her upstairs to rectify the situation and try and secure the deal. Maria would make a stream of mistakes but was jostled by the other to rectify the situation – to clean up the split milk.

Some of my colleagues felt sorry for me, and it became hard for me to see their pain. Michelle was tearful, and then I felt sorry; the book was not about bringing pain or humour but self-awareness.

John said, "I do not feel sorry for her. It is not my life; it is hers. But we can learn from it."

I liked this. I wanted others to learn from my story, but I knew I had no control over what any reader learned or desired to learn. I was looking forward to creating a passion in individuals, inspiring them to embody that passion in their daily lives. I recalled Roland Barthes' "Death of the Author", in which he argues that the onus of producing meaning is placed upon the reader. The author and reader part ways, and the text take on a life of its own in the reader's consciousness. This is a chance to choose a different reaction, and a different response. In you, there will be an awakening to do something so passionate that it has a ripple effect on the lives of others. It is an influence that is seen but also felt as a vibration.

The ultimate act was the unauthorised circulation of my personal journal to my former sister-in-law. From there, it would be passed to Andrew, and a few other sister-in-laws would jump on the bandwagon to circulate it further. Instinctively, I knew the threats would come. "You are not going to get away with saying all this about my family." I had twelve years of slanderous name calling about my family and the one-offs perturbed him.

Unfortunately, I could no longer be anonymous, and my manuscript's distribution alerted Andrew that the book existed. Now I risked not only making Andrew irate but causing the extended community to fume on the sidelines. I hoped that they believed in the greater good for the book.

When I confronted John about how the book had made its way to my former sister-in-law, he merely fudged. "What book?" he said. "You are writing a book?"

"You are as bad as them," I retorted. Upset, I left work early and later received an email telling me to go home and return with a medical note saying I was fit enough for work. John wanted to escape the confrontation and wanted to play neutral.

The distribution of the book to my former in-laws did not help matters. I braced myself for the threatening calls and emails I knew I'd receive. I did not account for the nail in my tyre, and when I went to see Andrew, I cried again. There seemed no end to the lengths they would go to. He could not support me openly, as his loyalty was to his family.

Fortunately, I was renting a room to Anselm, who had to come back to Canada. He was in the car and some noise told him something was wrong with the car. He also felt the difference as we drove and told me to pull over so he could look at the tyres. I had been oblivious to the noise or movement of the car.

Instinctively, I knew it was Andrew. Still, more importantly, I knew the intent for the act belonged to others.

As I drove after Anselm had put the spare tyre on, I noticed Andrew approaching the driveway. I parked. I saw a knowing smirk cross his face, and I knew it was Andrew. After everything I had undergone, this hurt me. Andrew was raised to do all the fighting for the family; what the others lacked courage to do, they assigned him to do. If they put the gun in his hand and asked him to shoot, he would hesitate, but he would do it. He would lie, cheat, steal, and kill just for the family. With the order from the family, he mentally abused me. With the order from the family, he blew my tyre. Everyone in the community said that, if you took him away from the family he was a good guy. But the family did not want him to be away; nor did he want to be away from them.

Going to work became harder, and I went to visit my former psychiatrist to see if I could get a medical note that would allow me to stay home. after The psychiatrist refused my request and my family doctor was only willing to give me a note to cover the number of days I had as sick leave. I could not play the system. While Andrew was using my illness as an alibi to get away with his family's dark hidden secrets, I wanted to see if I could get time off work because the environment had become toxic but even my psychiatrist was reticent. Strange, I could not even use their own diagnoses to get a year sick pay.

I stayed away from work. I enjoyed being with my son and focusing on my book and the people in my world. Going to work and pushing paper, like Papa's factory assembly line job, was a tiresome task. I had my own ambitions and my own passion.

Thankful for all my colleagues' comments during the impromptu book review, I began rewriting my book. I undertook all their questions and attempted to answer them.

To publish or not? Publish was Jenny's voice from London. If you can save and help one person, then it is worth it. I had wasted so many things in my life – my youth, my time, my energy – in the pursuit of worthless endeavours; I did not want to waste the book. These lives lived and their pain should not be taken for granted. This book did not deal with abuses alone; it dealt with the balance of greed, selfishness, envy, ego and vanity that can hurt a person. In this respect, the cause was universal and our identification inclusive. Not everyone suffers or witnesses abuse, but anyone interested can help.

Uzma, a Muslim girl who shared my journey at work, was very motivational. She offered her services as a publicist, and she spent her time researching how to advance and promote the book. In her, I saw how my story interconnected and was interwoven with hers. We shared similar paths, receiving our Canadian citizenships and getting our permanent jobs at close to the same time, and our personal struggles also resembled each other.

With the book in draft format and in circulation, "others" wanted to say, "But I did help her, and I did not do it for a name." Yes everyone helped at one point or another but not with the truth, which would have saved us all a lot of bother and I would have believed they actually cared.

With the book in a draft format, I remembered the fear of the "aunties" in the community, who did not want to spill anything else for fear that they too would find themselves in the book.

They said, "What is the point of talking to her? She is not saying anything."

These aunties, knowing of the nail in the tyre, were afraid that, if they said anything, they would receive a similar treatment. Nobody wanted to be caught making the statement, "He is an abused homosexual." The only comments I ever heard among the community were remarks such as, "You are too naive," in reference to my homosexual husband, or, "Well, at least she is out of the marriage." I thought of the worthlessness of a community of any kind if there is no one to tell you the truth and everyone is willing to act as a bystander to someone's pain. And it is sad when a community, instead, steps forward only to gossip, like vultures feeding on the carcasses of a failed marriage, the pain of another.

Could people unlearn what they knew? Could I learn something new? I knew that I had tried to be a high-society socialite, but one could not make a silk purse out of a sow's ear, though the in-laws had tried. Could this book create a house of butterflies? I had envisioned a house of butterflies as a metaphor; it's a building in which people can heal and move forward from past hurts – a safe haven where they can explore a vast array of possibilities. I wanted to see human beings having a second opportunity for a transformation – to see a broken person become one of strength, filled with happiness.

I pondered my own negligence, and I came up with the two-second rule, which I got from the rules of driving. The two-second rule suggests that we should keep our distance on the road of life when it comes to revenge, vengeance, retaliation, and vindictiveness. I also considered how one might curtail the awakening of a stirring of destruction and came up with the idea of visualising a man holding a gun (the oppressor) and the receiver of the bullet (the disempowered). As readers, we can suspend our disbelief and just image a reversal of roles to make the best decision. *There but for the Grace of God go I.*

Second Experts:
The Challenger

hankfully, I had an opportunity to seek another opinion, and I
asked my counsellor to recommend the best psychiatrist in town.

I made an appointment and again rolled off the list of events in
my life. When the one-hour session concluded, I asked for my diagnoses.

The psychiatrist with a large personality told me, "I have no
diagnoses for you."

Whoa! I was mentally liberated. Not believing this, I said, "I am
sensitive, and I hate watching murder and killing."

He did not feel that there was anything wrong with this. He asked
if I heard the TV or radio speak.

My reply was an emphatic, "No".

I mentioned the various scenarios of the who-is-Kumar's-
grandmother episode and my unhelpful schizo-affective disorder label
and the nail in the tyre. He replied, rather comically, "I have often
imagined an Italian nail."

I said, "Well, I have the nail, so I am not imagining this." Maybe this
was a simple test to see what I would have to say about the physicality
of the object or more importantly, he too as a professional knew the
difference between someone using someone's mental disposition to "get
away" with a wrongdoing.

He just laughed, advising me not to leave my journal in the printer
next time.

I replied, "I get it, and I know. But it is hard to clean up the split milk."

But I had to forget the spilt milk.

The psychiatrist went on to say that I sucked at judging men and advised that, next time, I should take my new man to see my counsellor, Dr Gilbert.

Next time, I was going to pay attention to the signs and would not be swayed by a crowd or the inconvenience of changing my course of life. I would follow the compass set by a predetermined destiny I had known as a child.

As I left the doctor's office, I said, "I am normal then?"

He waved me out of his office and said, "Whatever normal is!"

Forgiveness –
The Grace of God

Now, dear reader, you find that I should be angry with and unforgiving of Andrew for his deception, his lies, his act of damaging my tyre, the mental and emotional abuse I endured at his hands, and the wasted twelve years of my life.

I was saddened by his wasted life, by the years he'd robbed himself of with me. And now I had come to understand that he had not really had a life of his *own* or a life with me. I saw his torture; his purgatory on earth; and the tears that he shed in isolation at night, in the garage, and at times at the lake while he was fishing. I saw his isolation as he sent me to parties without him, as he brooded at home, as he struggled to come to terms with all he had needlessly undergone.

He wore the cloth of shame that was not his but that of his family and community. I saw a man who unselfishly tried to be anything other than what nature intended him to be. He did this all for the sake of his mother, brothers, sisters, nephews, and nieces. He thought he could protect Kumar, our son, and me with lies.

My wrath turned more now to his brothers, his sisters, his mother, his aunties and uncles and his cousins, and the extended community, who allowed his pain and his selfless giving to go on for so long and allowed him to walk alone on this path. What a living hell it must be – to never be true to yourself, to never be accepted by those who profess to love you, and to not be free to love who you want to love. He stood beside his family for far too long, but *none of them* stood beside

139

him. How dare you all ask your brother to sacrifice what you dared not sacrifice yourself, not for a day, a month, a year, or a lifetime? He would not have asked a sacrifice so great from any of you.

He carried his repentance for all of them. He wore the sins of his brothers and sisters because it was not his own intention to blow my tyre and mentally abuse me. They all pushed his hand into the fire, and they did not do it for the sake of Andrew. I held them all accountable and knew that Andrew had earned his place at a banquet far greater at a higher level.

I prayed that, when blessings came to him, his family would dare not take them from him. The family had already taken more than a lion's share of his life. What he had earned from heaven would be his by merit by the heavens. He, himself, was no less a child of God or lesser than them.

Some have cried on their wives' and husbands' shoulders like babies for their own hurts and pain, yet they denied their brother the opportunity for comfort, happiness, and a choice of partner. Water was the healer, the calming soothing balm, where he could be who he really was and at peace. It was as if the calming noise of the rippling water, and the stillness of nature had the ability turn the hot-head into a cool-head, I suspect it was because he needed the patience to hook the worm and catch the fish that lead him to still his mind.

Again I was angry, the wrath I had felt resurfaced, together with a choir of angels. I wanted to say to Andrew's family and community, "You denied your brother his own life – his own free will to choose his own actions, to heal, and to have his journey as was written by his stars - for God created the stars. A right to your own your life and free will is the only possession worthy on earth to earn your place in heaven.

"You must all, as a community, make recompense if you wish to make amends and atone for the sin of neglect of Andrew, for you all had a part, a share in his suffering by blocking his healing and denying him a voice.

I recalled the bible story about a woman who bled for twelve years, and she was courageous enough to touch Jesus, for healing. What progress for the Dark Ages. Though his pain was entrenched, Andrew could be healed. I knew that those who did not love and accept him as who he was would surely face a greater slap from heaven. If stones were thrown at him, rocks would boomerang into their lives. He deserved to be happy.

If, as a homosexual, you are not welcome, dust your feet at the foot of the door and walk on by; you are still a child of God. To love freely without coercion is to love purely; whether you love a man or a woman, the purity of love is that which is given freely. You are not alone; others go before you and after you, but with courage, you become an ambassador of the purity of free will and love – that is the divine. The body is either cremated or buried, but the spirit lives on for eternity, and it is the spirit that loves.

If I hadn't gotten out of my marriage when I did, I knew my in-laws would have carried on the games, and it would have destroyed me. If they were sorry, they would have stopped the mind games. I knew they were not truly repentant because they did not turn their back on the old ways of behaving and begin anew; they did not cease doing the wrongdoing. I suspected that they were sorry for all the wrong reasons. Unfortunately, since I left, I took away Andrew's family's opportunity to be repentant by their own choice. What remained was atonement of the sin – to begin anew, to abhor past actions and change. There is a higher celestial court that sees the hearts of men and women. Whenever I could not forgive, I handed it to God and asked for his grace of forgiveness.

I pondered over the Bible's words, "Do unto others as you will have them do unto you." Would my mother-in-law or my sister-in-law ever want to have a life like mine? Would they want to live with an abused homosexual and not be told why he was angry? I looked back into the past and saw that neither one of them flinched but stood firm on their ground that deluding me was acceptable. So effortlessly, the younger brother-in-law, Mark, said, "I stand by my sister because she is my sister."

How careless! They had their own daughters, who had to face the possibility of being someone else's sister-in-law, someone else's daughter-in-law. It is far better to stand by truth, justice, and fairness, failing which; you will receive the same injustice as that bestowed upon another. To do unto others as you would have them do unto you is a lesson worthy of repetition. Otherwise, you will be in danger of letting a petulant child and an even-toned voice be the guide of your conscience. You need only live by your own conscience and not by your brother's or sister's, for you alone will meet God on Judgement Day.

The anger resurfaced every time she saw them. It triggered the hurt all over again. Relationships, if they are destructive, will take you far from God, especially if you are far from loving and accepting yourself. I felt sorry for my nieces, sorry for their future, sorry that they would be disappointed, sorry they would be disillusioned by life. If their fathers, their own uncles and aunties, people from their own race in the extended community were part of the scheme that caused so much pain and destruction not only for me but Andrew too, I was saddened for a future generation. Who could they rely upon?

A Life of One's Own

With Ammah tucked safely away in the afterlife and with the end of my marriage, I could finally be responsible for my own life, my own choices, my own friends, and my own mistakes – and ultimately, my own destiny. I no longer wanted to play the roles other people wanted me to play; I was emotionally damaged and brutalised by others' lies and deception. I was at last not a pleaser, finally not a doormat.

Jenny from England helped me and coached me on the sidelines to fight for my rights and if I could not fight, then there is always someone who can fight for me. I could and did fight for my rights. I would evaluate the potential risk for further damage to human beings and sometimes let things go, knowing as always that life was the teacher. I would still be tenacious, and what I'd gone through might have caused others to crumble, but resolve and a streak of my father's determination had kept me going.

In the lull on my early days after my separation, I received an anonymous call asking for Kamala, my mother, and instinctively, I knew it was *them*. They were paying back for my exit out of the family and the marriage. Ammah in their mind, had not really helped me when I had Kumar or visited me more often. They assumed that one of the reasons why I left the marriage was because of the pain and suffering Ammah had undergone with their games, they steered Ammah to believe I was really sick and would succumb to the same fate as Fathima. I suppose Ammah's suffering was a contributing factor for leaving my marriage, it was not the sole one. In Jessie's and my mother-in-law's perception, I was leaving my marriage for a mother who did nothing for me.

I was disappointed again at their short-sightedness, visibly Ammah was a broken person, I could not see my issues with her. But then again, what could I expect from my in-laws, they had the same short-sightedness at their own brother and his pain. She could not fight for herself, let alone for me. More importantly, I saw the years I lost when I could have done things for my mother as a lost opportunity, I was in a bad marriage.

I pondered why they felt I did not have a mother's love, when surely we are mirror images of each other (daughter and mother), giving and taking. In my perception, sometimes as a child matures and a mother ages, the depth of a mother's love is the way a child loves his or her mother. In this respect, I think that nothing speaks more of a mother's love than a daughter or son's love. I mean, we see beyond our issues, if only to be giving rather than taking. I had the love of my mother; I had learnt from my mother to love another like a mother. Ammah was generous in spirit. I learnt to love all the elderly like my own, for failing to do so would have meant that I had forgotten to love my mother.

Angry about such a call, I attempted to get even. I decided I would stop them so they could never get to me again. Francine, my friend and I decided to get even. She pretended to be another child in search of her father and she called Celine. She was looking for my father-in-law. I staged the call and had no time to stop it.

As I went to Andrew's house, I wanted to stop my friend from calling but the call had already been placed. I saw my mother-in-law's *look* but only I said to my mother-in-law, "Truth lives no matter who dies, Ammah, you or I." I wanted her to know that you cannot escape.

I had reached the extent of my cruelty, and though there is no justification or excuse for what I did, I can only explain that I was motivated by feeling that my former in-laws should bear the brunt of a cruel intention. My only explanation is that, as a victim of psychological and emotional abuse, I had a right to be angry about all that was done to me.

Slowly, I began buying furniture, utensils, bedsheets, towels, and a lawnmower. I took my son's bed and assembled it in his room. The first summer was hot without an air conditioner, and the winter was dry without the humidifier. The winter was hard because I had to shovel the snow. I forgot all about the steps leading up to the front door, and a small mountain formed. I was thankful for my neighbours, who helped me that harsh winter. The stiffness of arthritis meant I needed more time in the morning to loosen the joints, and I felt the cold and pain shoot through my legs. Yet, where there was a pulse and a heartbeat, there was life.

At night-time, the bedbugs had a feeding frenzy, as flakes of dry skin fell upon my new bed; I scratched my legs incessantly at night, and my mouth was parched dry. The next year, I bought a humidifier; moisture returned indoors, and my skin glowed. The second summer, I installed an air conditioner, but it was not the Indian hot summer I had experienced the first year and, perhaps, not such a cost-effective expense.

I screwed up with Rogers Wireless, signing up for a one-year contract, and my bills were high. But I bought an iPhone 4. Balram and Hamza had had the iPhones 1, 2, and 3, but I had only had discovered the iPhone 4. I learnt that texting was the rage. I switched to a data plan and downloaded GasBuddy, an application on the new phone that depicted locations where I could buy cheap gas. It was a far cry from the time when I had signed a fixed contract with Enbridge at a higher price and Andrew had wanted me to go to my psychiatrist and get a letter to say that I was "schizo-affective" so I could get out of the contract. Now I owned my own mistake and did not need an alibi. I was doing well as an independent woman.

It was lonely at first, losing everyone all at the same time. I grieved the separation, and tears fell unashamedly in solitary isolation. It was a stressful year; I had grieved Ammah, the loss of a family, and an end of a marriage. My beautiful house, with all its modern conveniences, was a haven, and I had everything my heart ever desired. I was spoilt and blessed. Still, on the weeks I did not have my son, it was lonely. I was used to having the frills of my former extended family, all those extras.

My new place felt like a house, until I bought a puppy, a mix breed of shih-tzu and Chihuahua, and called him Butterscotch; he was a new companion for the road ahead. He had doll-like eyes that blinked and a face that stayed the same. Yet in him, I found a look that accepted a higher purpose; he was able to bring laughter and unity to people. I saw in his doe-eyed eyes love and devotion; he was uncannily human. In him, my son found a four-legged brother, and together they would play hide-and-seek, fight, and sleep in a makeshift tent.

Butterscotch would accompany me to school to meet Kumar. When the school bell sounded the end of the school day, the children would come to the gate to pet and cuddle Butterscotch, and they willingly offered themselves as dog sitters. Secretly, Kumar was indebted to Butterscotch, his four-legged brother, for a species of a different kind helped him find new friends at school.

I didn't hit the scenes of downtown Quebec, where everyone was so much younger. My walks around the pond were relaxing. I stood still, tilted my face to the sun, closed my eyes, and listened; the only noise in the background was the crickets and the whistling of wind through the trees. As I walked, I felt the rustling of the leaves as I stepped on the undergrowth. Looking up at the trees, I saw the leaves were the isolated wings of the butterfly, struggling to stay on the branches as the wind fought to take their fragility away. Like my spirit, at times the force of the family too threatened to take advantage of my fragility and I struggled to stay connected.

The only welcoming presence I felt was Kumar and Butterscotch beside me. Kumar was an avid explorer, who enjoyed his trips to the river, where he would roll up his trouser pants and walk bare feet on the rocks looking for crayfish and spottail shiners. Too many times in the water, and he soon succumbed to athlete's foot. Once or twice, he caught tadpoles and waited to see them turn into bullfrogs. Kumar gravitated towards the bridge and the water, just like his father. Kumar would once or twice dare me to walk upon the rocks as the current of the river flowed downstream and Kumar said. "You are a chicken, girls are!"

We would explore the surrounding nature trails. One day, we stumbled upon a nook by the stream and found remnants of a makeshift campfire – a dirty sleeping bag, torn candy wrappers scattered on the ground, plastic bags. I wondered what had happened the day before. Who had been there and what was his or her story? Teenagers enjoying nature I suspected. I had the time to imagine, to daydream and enjoy a reflective positive moment.

I began to fully appreciate my life in Canada and with each season, I watched the birds flock in line formation from north to south, flapping their wings furiously to keep in flight, to keep aligned. They woke me in the mornings when they tweeted and honked noisily.

I found a new church, one that had a mission component to it and wasn't a Catholic church, and attended Mass on Sunday. There I found a new community. Now I had two communities – the one I'd found on my walks around the pond, where the dog owners congregated, and the other at church.

One day, when attending a Christian talk, I heard the lecturer pipe on about how Muslims were converting killing machines who needed to be saved. I had my own Muslim sisters, who followed the path of God and not a definition of religion; they followed their own personal relationship with God and their own consciences. I happily, as a Catholic Christian, walked out of church that day and felt good about my decision because I knew my Muslim sisters would do the same for me. My own decision played out, and I was confident it was the right one.

As I walked my dog and found my community, I remembered Ammah and her walks to church with Fathima, Hamza, and myself all jostling her along each time she was cornered by someone with a heart-wrenching story. Butterscotch barked to move me along to where his buddies waited for him.

I was a sentimental and nostalgic person by nature; I would think that the mental abuse was sustainable. Each day came and went, until I realized that I was exhausted and drained. Safe in my own home, I knew that I could not go back. I had done the best I could. I no longer wanted to be afraid and lash out in anger. And as difficult as it was to forgive my in-laws' deception, I came back to two essential questions: Why were they doing this to me? And how could they do this to someone who was suffering? To know human pain is to alleviate the other's suffering. I asked why it was important to live a lie and how someone could watch a human being suffer and continually to deal out mental cruelty.

I thought about my past, when it had been raining men. These days, middle age was a nice way to avoid the "getting out there". I now had two chins instead of one, and my abdomen swelled to such a point that people would offer their seats on the bus for me. A swollen uterus; a bad-tempered gut; and breasts that were spreading north, south, east, and west were definitely forcing me to accept my age. My hair colour was left to the discretion of my stylist who, at the moment, was experimenting with highlights and tones of brown. She looked at magazines of stars and replicated them, and I sat there like a stool pigeon. My glasses were the brand name DKNY and discoloured by overuse or carelessness because Butterscotch enjoyed chewing the handles.

I looked back at how far I'd come – how I'd become my own person and taken the steps to return to an essence of myself, a wiser self. I was happy that I was not naive anymore. Now in my late forties, I wasn't willing go back to being a romantic wearing "rose-tinted glasses", where the world was idyllic and full of promise. I saw my world as full of possibilities of my own creation. I was free of medication, and I wasn't seeing any counsellors or psychiatrists. I still carried the scars internally and sometimes still was afraid and stressed about the will of man to inflict pain upon another.

The Lessons

*I*n the end, the lesson I learnt was that "home" was neither England nor Canada. Nor could it be found in running away and looking outside myself for strength. I had to understand myself first and make a decision. Home was not crying in a car park in Quebec or going to a friend's house for a momentary escape. Home was where I could sleep without checking over my shoulder, listening to conversations, and figuring out the other side's game plan.

"Home" now was anywhere in the world, as long as I could be at peace. It was where I could cook what I wanted to eat, sleep when I wanted, and dress exactly as I saw fit. It was where I was free to have takeaway instead of cooking dinner, and where, if I didn't want to do the housework, I just relaxed. Home was where I could be a slob and no one would say anything about it, where I could pick my nose and no one would report publicly that I had done so. I was free to own my own mistakes and my own choices, good or bad, and no one was there to tell me where I'd gone wrong all the time. I owned it.

I now understood that the greatest possession anyone could own was a right to his or her own life. There was no need to respect someone else's timeline or to march to a rhythm of life other than my own. After years of thinking that I was not "good enough" or successful enough, I realised that my journey and success meant fulfilling my own destiny, my own vision and dream. Mine may not be the dream of the other, but it was just as important, just as self-fulfilling. It was a wilting dream, reviving in the wake of this book.

Now my purpose was to help others alleviate their suffering – to help them make choices that would boost their mental and physical health.

They would be able to handle their chronic and physical conditions because the stress of a bad marriage was no longer pushing them to experience these conditions at a high level.

I was looking forward to the return of the angel, the essence of soul that would always choose to have empathy for others' pain. I was hopeful that, in the future, I would begin to trust again, begin the journey to return to the self that I loved, a self that was the balm and anointment on human pain, rather than the darker side that poured acid on a wound with words. I was hopeful for a transformation of the moth, spiritual and beautiful, transcending all hurts, and free. Bitterness would be past and would no longer threaten to consume me like a match to a cardboard box. I would be able to be strong with anyone who attempted to hurt me, safe with the knowledge that some people needed to lie for their survival, whereas others needed truth for their survival.

I knew that the lessons of culture and religion *could be* repressing. However, like the onion peel, there were layers and layers of universal shared truths that allowed people to see beyond the differences to draw everyone closer to humanity. I will always be a Tamil girl by blood, distant at times culturally from my Sri Lankan roots and my native birthplace, Malaysia. The exposure of living in England, Malaysia, and now Canada made a wonderful combination. Like a sweet and sour Chinese dish or gravy for a bland roast or a hot sauce for fish and chips, each culture was complementary to one another, each enhancing the taste of the other. Unravelling the onion peel that sheltered the core of every human being was worth the effort, as it allowed you to know and appreciate that person.

I needed no sari to be Tamil and no gold to be a rich Tamil. I was no less of a Tamil because others saw me as diluted and impure in my roots. How they viewed me and how I fancied myself were yards apart. I was comfortable in my skin, the skin of my year. I had shed what I saw as irrelevant and unimportant and owned the right to decide.

When a helper came to my door, I never asked what his or her religion was but said, "Thank you, God, for sending me someone, and bless you for coming."

I came to understand that I could not go down other people's past paths to heal the hurts they'd encountered and right the wrongs they'd be done in their lives. Finally, I accepted that I could not stop the glass from falling and shattering into pieces and I could not waste my time or energy trying to change that which was already done.

I was the captain of my own destiny. I was an artist, like Raphael, in front of a blank canvas. And I would paint my future with bright colours of hope, faith, and charity. I did not want to see my life in any other way. Now, I fancied Andrew as "the fisher king".

Others saw my life differently and questioned my motives. But in the end, I had to fulfil my karmic duty, as my destiny was written in my stars. Just for once, if only in a book, I cared not what others thought. I was that good and I was that bad; but whatever I was, I owned the right to decide. I was doing well for someone who was *that sick*. Or maybe I was not that sick at all.

Afterword

This book began as a personal journey for healing, for grieving, and for releasing the past. I encountered so many blocks as I attempted to "let go", including the desire to please my father and mother and then entering and staying in a bad marriage. Isn't it sad that what a reader may take away from the book is the date with the stripper or my relationship with a married man? You would have missed the whole point if you allowed yourself to be distracted by trivial nonsense, but then again, you would have had to care for my struggles and that of Andrew and my child. Society's values are all messed up.

On my road to recovery, I met so many people who were suffering from abuses during their childhood – a father who had to come to terms with his son abusing his daughter; a niece who was abused by her uncle; and grandchildren who, as adults, had to "let go" of abuses dealt to them as children by their grandfathers. This book had to be shared universally because, even if you are not subjected to abuse or a witness to abuse, suffering abuse is universal. Deciding to take the step-by-step progress from victim to survivor is a hard choice to make, but in isolation, abuse festers and is an open wound.

In coming to terms with my past, I have finally reunited with my sister who passed away, knowing that she will always be with me. So often, we can feel dispersed, isolated in our own experience. We think that it's unique. But we are not alone; others have had similar journeys. By sharing my story, I wanted other fathers and mothers to know they are not alone when they find themselves caring for their mentally ill children.

Finally, so ends a love story of a different kind – that of a Tamil homosexual and a coconut.

Edwards Brothers Malloy
Oxnard, CA USA
June 6, 2014